FOOD FiGHT!

Volume 1

FOOD FiGHT!

Volume 1

David Butteridge

Brick By Brick Press

For Grandad.

Because of Harri.

"Marvellous" Marvin Bagel versus "King"
Cassius Cake

Undoughsputed

Champion versus Champion

WAFFLE: We are into the final three rounds here and there is still very little to separate these two distinguished boxers as we look to crown the first ever undisputed champion in the history of the Doughjo.

Of the two, it's the BUN FiGHT! Champion, "Marvellous" Marvin Bagel, who leads on my scorecard by just a single round from nine - but don't count out the prodigious talent of the FOOD FiGHT! Champion, the boxer formerly known as Cassius "Birthday" Cake, who came back from the brink to win the title against Frank Chouxno exactly one year ago today.

If you're just joining us - where have you been? Alongside me, Walter Waffle, are Rick Roll and

Lennon Drizzle, and we have witnessed an incredible night of action so far. Which way do you see this going as we enter the championship rounds, chaps?

ROLL: Bagel for me, Wally. He's got the durability, he's got the power - one good punch is all he needs to end this, and he's not far from landing it.

DRIZZLE: Are you kidding me? Bagel's been hit all night and every which way. He's got to be at least three rounds behind. Sure, he's taking the hits well - but Cake is something else. He's quick, he's slick, and he's gonna win big.

ROLL: Three rounds? You know we're supposed to be unbiased, right?

DRIZZLE: I said what I said.

WAFFLE: It has been a real treat so far, no matter how you've scored it. A proper boxing contest. The raw power of Marvin Bagel, the toughness and bravery to keep coming forward, to keep advancing on his opponent. The swift feet and accurate counter-punching of the youngster, Cake, the ring awareness, the tactical mastery beyond his years. He may not have been in the game of pugilism for long but he has taken to it like no-one I've ever seen before.

DRIZZLE: Uncle Sponge taught him well, Wally. Watch him win it this round.

ROLL: Whereas Bagel had to learn in the ring,

build himself up from the bottom. There was no easy route for him just because of who he's related to.

WAFFLE: Both fighters are back to their feet, referee Mark Battenberg is looking over to the timekeeper and…

Ding!

WAFFLE: Here we go! Round ten of twelve in this absorbing, incredible contest between two of the Doughjo's finest, fiercest fighters.

It's Bagel making moves first, as he has been doing all match. Occupying the centre and marching forwards, slightly shorter reach but he's stocky, stout. Cake is keeping him at bay with those rapid-fire jabs, though. A couple of good ones landing there as he skirts around the edge of the ring, keeps his back close to the ropes.

Bagel with an attempt at a big left-hook but Cake takes it on the guard, not letting anything get through. Huge roar from the crowd here in the Bread Bin, the massive all-seater arena in the Breadinburgh district of this fine old bakery. It's home advantage for Bagel, and the fans are right behind him with every punch.

DRIZZLE: They obviously don't appreciate good boxing.

ROLL: What are you talking about? The sport was invented here.

WAFFLE: Oh! A clubbing right hook from Bagel gets through the guard. Cake's trying to smile it off but his eyes say that that really hurt. He'll be trying to catch his breath now.

Bagel doesn't give him a second, though. He's onto his opponent, combination shots and it's all Cake can do to cover up, to bob and weave. It's damage limitation.

Another big shot gets through - and another! Cake moves into a clinch and the referee, Battenberg, has to break them apart.

DRIZZLE: Smart from the young man, very smart.

WAFFLE: Can Cassius Cake make it out of this round? Bagel has started with a point to prove.

They come back together, Cake determinedly firing out his shots in response - fast, flashes of blue whizzing towards Bagel's face and body. An impressive feat of endurance and energy to throw these out after the barrage he just received. That being said, Bagel keeps walking through them, keeps tanking the hits to move in closer.

Cake clinches up again before any damage can be done and the crowd don't like this at all. Not at all. The boos rain down from the rafters.

ROLL: They came to see a fight, not a cuddle.

DRIZZLE: Goes to show you that hundreds of fans

can spend hundreds of tokens, and they still don't know a single thing about boxing.

ROLL: Oh, please.

DRIZZLE: Seriously. Cassius Cake is doing what needs to be done to win. If they don't like it, then I don't know what to tell them.

WAFFLE: Bagel charges in again after the break, and he throws another big right hand that- Oh! Cassius Cake returns fire and that one has caught Bagel flush, and he's stepping backwards for the first time in the match. Cake is advancing, capitalising on this rare moment where Bagel looks to be on jelly legs.

DRIZZLE: Get him!

WAFFLE: A straight left, a right, he's trying to probe around the older boxer's defence and he's finding the gaps - but has he got the power in these punches to knock Bagel down?

An explosion of energy from Cassius Cake, a flurry of strikes. Bagel's up against the ropes now and seems to have found some stability, he's offering a jab or two back in response but Cake senses that this might be his chance.

DRIZZLE: Finish it!

WAFFLE: Arms are up from Bagel, he's doing a good job of blocking, but Cake is relentless here. It's punch after punch against that glazed exterior. You can see the tears opening up on Bagel, you can see the soft white crumb exposed.

DRIZZLE: How's the ref not stepped in here? It's over. Call it off already!

WAFFLE: It's looking bad for Bagel here, can he res-

Ding!

DRIZZLE: No!

WAFFLE: That's the end of the round and, wow. It went back-and-forth, but you'd have to say that assault at the end from Cassius Cake probably tips it in his favour. This really is something. What a match!

DRIZZLE: That's it now. Cake's won this. He knows he can hurt Marvin Bagel and he'll finish it in the next round. Mark my words, Wally.

ROLL: Bagel just took the best Cake could offer and he's still in this. Still standing. He's had his wobble now.

WAFFLE: An incredible display from the FOOD FiGHT! Champion, still undefeated in his young career. This is his first fight outside of Calorifornia and he is justifying his considerable hype.

Marvin Bagel is being tended to by his team. They're egg-washing those rips and tears on his face and body. Giving him some advice, giving him time to breathe. Bagel's also undefeated but from twice as many fights. He's been here before. He's defending his championship for the thirteenth time, and a win will break the record for the most defences of all-time. A record that he currently shares with the BUN FiGHT! co-founder, "Brilliant" Breaderick Bun.

ROLL: An incredible boxer. Breaderick Bun really was brilliant. Turned up on the scene and he was the best thing since... Well, I don't know what.

WAFFLE: Both of the Bun brothers are in attendance tonight, of course, Breaderick Bun and his brother, "Iced" Finger Bun. The latter not only co-founded BUN FiGHT! but also set up the rival promotion, FOOD FiGHT!, to offer opportunities to a wider variety of fighters.

ROLL: Surprised to see them together after all the animosity. Imagine betraying your family like that.

DRIZZLE: Imagine betraying the rest of the Doughjo by only allowing savouries to fight. "Iced" Finger Bun is a hero and you lot in Breadinburgh should appreciate that FOOD FiGHT! has even bothered to turn up here.

WAFFLE: Well, a first-ever cross-promotional event and a fight between the two respective champions is a great first step towards harmony in the Doughjo, and I think we can all agree on that.

Whoever wins this fight will be champion of both promotions, becoming only the second fighter ever to have held both belts and the first to hold them both simultaneously. There is history on the line. Legacy. We've said it many times before: all it takes is one good punch to write your name into the record books.

Ding! Ding!

WAFFLE: The bell signals the start of the eleventh round of this twelve-round contest. The penultimate round.

On the left of your screens, it's "Marvellous" Marvin Bagel in black shorts with a silver trim and the black gloves.

On the right, "King" Cassius Cake wearing blue and pink shorts, and blue gloves. He approaches with his arms down, almost asking for Bagel to take a swing at him.

Bagel obliges, misses, and Cake gets a couple of easy jabs in. Cassius is mocking his opponent here, shuffling his shoulders. Laughing.
ROLL: He won't be for long. Sheer disrespect.
DRIZZLE: It's not disrespect, it's mind games. It's all part of the sport.
WAFFLE: It's having the desired effect, as Bagel takes another big swing and misses, gets caught with a reply. You can see the frustration on his face. In the build-up to this match, Cassius Cake

talked a big game, talked confidently of overcoming the one they call "Marvellous", played down Bagel's achievements, and that has got to be something that Bagel has in his mind.

ROLL: Oh, definitely. I know Marvin well and he will not have liked being dismissed.

WAFFLE: It's slowed down a bit here. Bagel not falling for Cake's ploy; Cake not changing tact. Is this a sign that both fighters feel they're ahead, Lennon?

DRIZZLE: Wally, it's a sign that Bagel knows he's done for. Can't hit Cassius, can't keep getting hit or he'll collapse. Look at the damage on him! Meanwhile, Cassius looks fresh.

ROLL: You just spout such nonsense, Lennon. Honestly.

DRIZZLE: If you can't see that I'm right, you need your eyes testing, Rick.

WAFFLE: Bagel lands with a jab but you have to praise the way Cassius Cake is dealing with the southpaw. With this match even so far, Cake is looking the more controlled in these final rounds. Careful, precise punches. No wasted effort.

Great example there as he nails a three-punch combination to Bagel as he tried to close in. He flicks those shots out with ease and, rather than get carried away, keeps to the outside. Keeps to his tactic.

ROLL: Bagel needs to find a way past this. The lad's playing for a points victory.

DRIZZLE: Cake's always looking for the knock-out, Rick. You watch, he'll get him.

WAFFLE: It's true that the majority of his wins have been by knock-out, and normally before the latter rounds. However, the same is true of Marvin Bagel, who does have the weight advantage in this match up despite being the smaller boxer. He's got density on his side but he hasn't made it count yet.

Although he comes forward here and cracks Cassius Cake with a massive straight right. Wow, that has Cassius on the back foot. Follows up with a jab, a second, and Cassius heads for the clinch - but Bagel's evaded it. Oh! That one went straight to the jaw, and another around the side of the head. Cassius Cake is unsteady, and there's an overhand shot to the other side.

DRIZZLE: No!

WAFFLE: Cake is bouncing off of the ropes, he's looking for refuge. The referee is having a look but it goes on with Bagel closing in again, with Bagel launching another shot, and another. Cassius can't run away fast enough!

The crowd are roaring "Marvellous" Marvin Bagel on. It is deafening in here, they're on their feet. The Bread Bin has come alive, come unhinged. This is it, surely? Cake can't even get his arms up as another two big shots come in, a third to the mid-section, a fourth to the gut.

ROLL: Referee's got to stop it here, Wally.

WAFFLE: Bagel, another big punch and Cake is slumping in the corner!

Ding! Ding!

ROLL: Yes! It's over: Bagel wins!

DRIZZLE: No!

ROLL: Wait, what? The referee called it off, didn't he?

WAFFLE: I'm not… I don't know. Battenberg is talking to the timekeeper and he's sending both fighters back to their corners. It looks like that was the bell for the end of the round.

ROLL: You're kidding me? Cake was out of it. He was gone.

WAFFLE: I'm sure you can hear them at home, but the boos are raining down. Cassius Cake is confused. Marvin Bagel is confused. The referee is confused. Heck, we're confused too. That surely wasn't a full three minutes?

ROLL: No chance. They've cut that round short, Wally.

DRIZZLE: Seemed like three minutes to me.

ROLL: Stop it, Lennon. Come on now.

WAFFLE: The referee is talking it over with the

timekeeper and the judges. They're still in animated conversation. Shrugs all around. Bagel is still arguing but he's being told to go back to his corner. He's furious!

ROLL: Wouldn't you be? He had it won there.

DRIZZLE: Never.

WAFFLE: Cassius Cake was certainly looking worse for wear as he staggered back to his corner. He'll welcome the break. But just how close was he to being stopped?

DRIZZLE: Nowhere near and any one of these, frankly, idiots who thinks he was about to lose need to get outside more. He had Bagel right where he wanted him.

ROLL: Bagel pummelled him and I can't believe the ref didn't get in there sooner. He was done for. The fans are booing because even they can see it from up there in the cheap seats!

Lennon, there's loyalty, and then there's making yourself look stupid. Come on, admit it: Cassius Cake just lost the match. Admit it.

DRIZZLE: Not a chance. Not. A. Chance.

WAFFLE: Well, whatever happened in the closing stages, I'm sure we'll find out after the match. There will have to be an inquest. That seemed like half a round to me.

DRIZZLE: Oh come on. Let the timekeeper do their job and stop being so biased.

ROLL: Ha! Unbelievable.

WAFFLE: While the boos are still pouring down, you have to say that this is still anyone's fight going into the final round. It's been an even contest and our commentary desk is split, with just a few rounds in it either way-

DRIZZLE: -Not for me. It's Cassius by a distance-

WAFFLE: -so it will come down to the final round. A showdown between two great champions with almost twenty combined defences between them. With history, with legacy on the line.

For the winner: it's immortality. The first fighter to ever claim to be the one true champion of the Doughjo. A crest of invincibility. A place in the hall of fame, in the pantheon of greats who have graced the squared circle. The right to be called "Undisputed".

For the loser: it's immortality of a very different kind. Forever known as the one who came up short in the biggest boxing match in history. Resigned to an eternity as the best of the rest.

Make no mistake, this is huge. The biggest three minutes in boxing history is upon us.

Both fighters are back to their feet, Cassius Cake looking a bit steadier now, as we head into the final round.

Ding! Ding! Ding!

WAFFLE: Here we go! Round twelve, the championship round. The deciding round. Fame. Infamy. Ignominy.

Marvin Bagel extends a glove of respect and-Oh! Cassius clobbers him. The boos are thunderous, but Cassius just swung for Marvin Bagel with a huge uppercut and it has sent him staggering backwards.

ROLL: Despicable!

DRIZZLE: Excellent!

WAFFLE: Cake holds up his hands but referee Battenberg is giving a standing count to Bagel, who seems fine. That will have riled him up, though. Wow. I have never seen that happen before.

DRIZZLE: An honest mistake, Wally.

WAFFLE: Be that as it may, the Bread Bin audience are furious and even the small pocket of support Cassius had is going to struggle to be heard amongst the cries for Marvin Bagel now.

They're coming back together and Cake extends the glove this time, which Bagel meets with a gentle bump. He seems to have accepted it was an error of judgement.

ROLL: Better than I would've done. I would've whacked him, Wally.

DRIZZLE: Oh I bet you would.

WAFFLE: He's charging forward though. Bagel, that is. Undeterred from that stunning opening shot, he's closing in as he did before. Keeping Cake's arms tight to his body, not letting him use the reach. He's laying in plenty of punches. Indefatigable. Defiant.

He's backed by the crowd, all stood on their feet. Cassius Cake is still moving, still swivelling away from the experienced fighter who grew up just down the aisle from this arena. Who achieved his dreams when he beat Nigel Bun all those years ago to become champion. Here he is, trying to unify the Doughjo.

Cassius Cake is not out of this yet, though. He's returning fire as best he can. Short, sharp shots back to the tears around Bagel's eyes, to the shoulders. Doing what he can to try and keep scoring, but Bagel has had the more impressive round so far, looks the busier of the two. Is that beating at the end of the last round still having an effect?

ROLL: Keep on him, Marv.

WAFFLE: The referee separates them again and we're back in the middle of the ring, but it's soon apparent that Cassius Cake wants to take this to the ropes. He backs up again, and Bagel isn't even pretending to dodge the punches. He's walking through them, firing back some of his own. Big, heavy-handed blows, landing with a thud. Look at the way Cassius' cupcake case is covered in fist marks.

Cassius returns fire with a good, solid straight, into a hook, keeps following up and Bagel is in reverse now. Another jab and- Oh! Bagel is down.

ROLL: He tripped him!

DRIZZLE: He's clobbered him!

WAFFLE: Marvin Bagel is indicating to referee Mark Battenberg that it was a trip, but Battenberg is giving him another standing count.

ROLL: Look at him, he's fine.

WAFFLE: Bagel does seem to be ok, it looked like a bit of a tangle of limbs - be it a trip or a slip - but "Marvellous" Marvin Bagel is protesting again about this.

You can understand his frustration given everything seems to be going against him right now. The last round, the punch at the start, and now this incident.

DRIZZLE: Are you serious? He's in a boxing ring and he's moaning about being hit. Give me a break.

WAFFLE: The referee rules he's good to continue and Bagel is going to have to re-focus here. By the book, that's two knock-downs against him this round and if the judges see it that way then Marvin Bagel's title defence could be in real trouble right now.

He shakes off a couple more punches, misses one of his own. By the way he's coming forward, he must feel like he's behind on the scorecards here.

ROLL: Or like he won't win without a knock-out. Something stinks about this fight.

DRIZZLE: Who's unbelievable now?

WAFFLE: Crunching shot to the body but Cake replies with a vicious punch to the head, and there's still nothing between these two warriors. They are going blow-for-blow, punch-for-punch. I don't see either being stopped here, they just keep on firing back at each other. If earlier in the fight was a testament to the precision and the beauty of this deadly dance, then this round is boxing as a fight, as an educated brawl. Thump or be thumped.

A lovely evasive manoeuvre - how many have we seen today? - from Cassius Cake. A sly jab, a shuffle around the ring. Bagel is keeping steady, that low and wide stance. He wants - perhaps needs - to end this with a knock-out. He's waiting for his moment.

We keep saying it but it remains true: one good punch, that's all it takes.

Pawing out with some jabs now from Bagel, not making much of it. The right hand moving a bit slower, but just trying to get Cassius to open himself up, to make a mistake. Every punch counts now, every block, every dodge. The smallest margins will be the difference between victory and defeat.

DRIZZLE: Crowd's quiet. Even his hometown can't stand to cheer for a loser.

WAFFLE: There's anxiety in the air, certainly. There are cheers for Bagel, but they are hopeful, nervous. They want to see one last flurry but they know that Cassius Cake has the potential, has the weaponry to surprise him as he lands another couple of jabs. Cake is still doing most of the moving, Bagel throwing fewer punches now but waiting. Biding his time.

It's suddenly got tense here and we are in the final throes of this contest. It has been round-for-round the entire time, nobody ever establishing themselves as dominant, nobody ever taking charge of the scorecards. Just when you think momentum's going one way, these great champions find a way to reverse it.

Bagel catches Cake with a solid straight but doesn't follow up. Cake counter-punches but it's a rare miss and he gets caught with a stiff jab.

ROLL: Was that the moment for Marvin?

WAFFLE: Time is ticking away here, and Bagel keeps his eyes fixed on Cassius Cake.

And now, he springs into action. He's going to

end this one slugging it out! A whirlwind of punches, his black-gloved fists are flying and Cassius has found himself backed into the corner, he's trying to cover u- No!

Cassius is firing back, and he's backing up the BUN FiGHT! Champion. Oh we can hear the punches as they land from here and they are heavy, heavy shots, landing on the body, hitting the face. There's no rhyme nor reason, it's a straight-up brawl between two of the finest fighters we have ever witnessed in the ring.

DRIZZLE: Get him, that's it!

ROLL: The body, Marv. The body!

WAFFLE: The fans are cheering, the noise is something like I've never experienced in all my years commentating on this beautiful, destructive sport.

This is something else and neither man looks set to fall as their punches slow but the weight of them is still there, still carrying through. Will either fighter falter before the bell? Has anyone got that knock-out power left in the final moments of the match?

Ding! Ding! Ding!

WAFFLE: Both throw their arms in the air to claim victory but this one will go to the judges at ringside. What do we think here, chaps?

DRIZZLE: Wow. What an atmosphere for a start.

WAFFLE: Is your voice ok, Lennon?

DRIZZLE: I might've lost it a bit there at the end, definitely. Wow. What a fight. Fair play to Bagel, he stood up and took those punches, threw some good stuff back at Cassius Cake, but it's Cake by four rounds for me. Minimum.

ROLL: It's never four rounds. I've got Bagel by one round. He took too many punches but his earlier work should see him through, and the fact is he had Cassius Cake down-and-out in the eleventh, and I can't believe the judges won't give him some credit for that.

WAFFLE: For what it's worth, I've got them at six rounds apiece for a draw.

DRIZZLE: Get off the fence, Wally!

WAFFLE: Sorry, Rick - I'd go for Cassius on the pure number of punches he landed but I think Marvin Bagel did the most damage out there. He'll wake up feeling fresher tomorrow.

DRIZZLE: He's torn to bits, Wally.

WAFFLE: I said 'fresher', not fresh. Both of these two champions will be feeling it for a few days, I'm sure.

While the judges confer, we see the Bread brothers make their way into the ring. Breaderick Bun is stood with his champion, and he looks pretty happy. "Iced" Finger Bun also looks relaxed, so even the two most powerful promoters in boxing seem to think their respective charge has done enough.

"Iced" Finger Bun just having a word with the master-of-ceremonies now. What a contrast, to see all the tuxedos and the suits, the crisp white shirts and polished shoes and dazzling smiles; and, alongside them, the battered and bruised, the exhausted expressions of the two gladiators, who are getting a rousing ovation from the fans.

This really was one of the best fights I have ever witnessed. It really was.

ROLL: No argument from me.

DRIZZLE: Nor me. It maybe needed a knock-out but the quality and the sheer will to win on both sides was just... wow. That's all you can say really.

ROLL: Wow, yeah. That's how I feel.

WAFFLE: We have witnessed something special tonight, that's for sure: Lennon Drizzle and Rick Roll agreeing on something.

ROLL: Ha! That's funny for you, Wally.

DRIZZLE: Very good.

WAFFLE: Now, what's going on here, then? They're clearing the ring. The referee is having a chat with Cassius and Marvin. Breaderick Bun looks absolutely furious, he's right in the face of his brother. Oh! He's just pushed him. "Iced" Finger

Bun has hit the mat; Breaderick Bun is now being escorted from the ring. What has happened here? I didn't see anything at ringside but, well, Breaderick Bun is apoplectic and he is shouting something to his brother, who doesn't seem to be taking any notice of it. "Iced" Finger Bun's smirking, even. What is going on here?

ROLL: He's saying his brother's a liar, I think. Looks like he wants Bagel to follow him out of the ring.

WAFFLE: Silence descends over the crowd as BUN FiGHT! co-founder and commissioner, Breaderick Bun, is removed from the arena but what made him flip a switch like that?

Well, as a fighter, he was always known to be cool and calm under pressure but it has boiled over here in this clash of champions. Marvin Bagel is still in the ring, he looks confused but he's still in the ring.

What is happening here at the end of this epic bout? What a shame that these scenes may detract from the spectacle we have been treated to.

ROLL: Seems like they're going to keep fighting, judging by the way they're limbering up again.

DRIZZLE: Have you ever seen this before? This is a first for me.

WAFFLE: Now, hold on. I'm just getting word through my earpiece that there will be a thirteenth and final round. Apparently, the judges had this match as a draw but "Iced" Finger Bun has demanded a conclusion. It will be a single-round shoot-out.

ROLL: Can he do that?

WAFFLE: He's the FOOD FiGHT! commissioner and founder, and the fight is under FOOD FiGHT! rules so... I don't know but I suppose so. It's unprecedented, but I suppose so.

DRIZZLE: It doesn't matter if he can. He is doing it now. It's happening.

WAFFLE: And if you at home can hear boos, that is the crowd reacting to this announcement as it is being delivered through the speakers here. "Iced" Finger Bun isn't going to have many friends left in Breadinburgh after this. They seem to think Marvin Bagel is being cheated out of the win.

DRIZZLE: Most unusual this, Wally, but do any of us really want to see a draw today? Isn't this good?

ROLL: So why wasn't this stipulated ahead of time? They both went all in on that last round to win and there's another chance? I don't know, this doesn't seem right.

WAFFLE: Well, right or not: it is happening.

The ring is clear now, just "Marvellous" Marvin Bagel and "King" Cassius Cake, alongside the referee. Another three minutes for one of them to take home all the gold, all the glory.

Neither boxer is in their best shape. The flamboyant, vibrant pink-and-white icing and golden-brown sponge of Cassius is punctured, is beaten and stretched. The tough, glazed exterior of his opponent, Bagel, ripped and torn, dripping with egg-wash to try and keep him in this, try and hold him together for one last round.

The crowd is a cacophony of cheers for Bagel, the hometown hero. There are boos as well - perhaps not directly for Cassius Cake, the champion who has made this fight such a spectacle, but for what he represents. For who he represents. DRIZZLE: "Iced" Finger Bun doesn't look too upset, does he?

Ding!

WAFFLE: The thirteenth round of twelve begins. Surely the final round, but who knows at this point? Both fighters touch gloves without incident this time in a humbling show of sportsmanship.

I'm being told that the rest of the fight's scoring won't be taken into account. It's just on this round should we get to points. So, it's three minutes to be busy, to make your shots count.

Which way is it going to go, Rick? ROLL: I have to say, I don't like this for Marvin Bagel. It feels like this fight's against him, he's got to know that. He's keeping his distance here but he needs a knock-out to win, and I don't think he's going to get it.

WAFFLE: Lennon Drizzle?

DRIZZLE: Cassius Cake on points. He's too good across a single round. He just is.

WAFFLE: Marvin Bagel is on the outside now, but Cake doesn't move in to engage. They're circling from a distance and, with so much on the line, it's understandable.

Bagel is still doing the chasing but at a slower pace, trying to reach with a jab, trying to keep his right arm primed and ready to use to devastating effect. But Cassius is wise to it, and he'll keep trying to find the jab when he can.

It's Cassius who lands the first, and second. Three quick jabs, doesn't follow up. Skittles backwards, so light on his feet.

And that seems to have given Marvin Bagel an excuse to rush him. Oh! Bagel slugs a huge haymaker, misses, and Cassius has caught him again and lands a big uppercut of his own. Cassius in pursu- Oh no! Bagel does hit with the haymaker this time and Cassius is rocked, he's on the ropes. Bagel coming in hot but he gets caught twice more, and another big uppercut sends him wobbling.

ROLL: Unreal.

WAFFLE: Cassius Cake advancing. Jab, straight.

He's on to him now and sends a punch right through the middle of Bagel and he thumps into him. Bagel's down.

ROLL: He's giving him a count. Are you seeing this, Wally? This ref is crooked!

DRIZZLE: Did Cake punch him then? Or was it just a collision?

WAFFLE: Hard to see but the referee is giving his third count of the match to Marvin Bagel, who went down in a heap in what we thought to be a collision between the two. It looked to me as though Cassius Cake tried for that uppercut again, missed it and went through the hole in the middle of Marvin Bagel, which then carried him into his opponent.

Either way, Bagel is back up, but that took a chunk out of his chin. That is nasty.

ROLL: I can't believe he got a count for that.

WAFFLE: They restart and Bagel is on the attack but he's not steady on his feet here. He hits a nasty hook but he's almost fallen over himself.

Cassius Cake now hits back, two good shots to the body.

DRIZZLE: Go for the head!

WAFFLE: Marvin Bagel isn't defending himself well, and these punches to the head are landing without reply. This doesn't look good for the reigning BUN FiGHT! Champion at all. He gets a left of his own in but- Oh! He's down, Bagel is down!

Cassius Cake lamped him with a third devastating uppercut, right to that huge wound under his jaw, and he crashes to the canvas.

Referee's up to five but Bagel is on his feet. He's being checked over.

ROLL: No way.

WAFFLE: That's it-

DRIZZLE: -Yes!-

Ding! Ding! Ding!

WAFFLE: It's over: Cassius Cake is the winner by knock-out.

Cassius Cake is the new undisputed champion of the Doughjo. The referee has seen enough and, though Marvin Bagel is still protesting, he was wobblier than a jelly on a plate at the end.

ROLL: Now we know why Breaderick Bun was so angry. He could see it was a fix.

WAFFLE: It ends in unfortunate circumstances with a clash of bodies seemingly doing enough to rock Marvin Bagel in the last round, the thirteenth round. But there can be no doubt now as Cassius Cake is lifted on the shoulders of his team. FOOD FiGHT! Champion and, now, BUN FiGHT! Champion. The first to hold both belts simultaneously.

Cassius Cake is undisputed. *Undoughsputed.*

Spare a thought for Marvin Bagel, who still can't believe it. He's still protesting the result, the first loss of his esteemed career, ending his reign at twelve defences, but what a moment for Cassius Cake.

DRIZZLE: Huge, huge moment. Even if the crowd want to try and ruin it with their boos. Trust me when I say that everyone back home in Calorifornia will be very, very happy for Cassius Cake.

WAFFLE: A moment of real quality and, in the end, that uppercut did for Marvin Bagel. One good punch, we've said it so often. One good punch. That was the difference between these two gladiators this evening.

Cassius Cake lifts aloft the BUN FiGHT! and FOOD FiGHT! belts, "Iced" Finger Bun is in there as well to celebrate with his charge. What a momentous moment for this young prodigy, a boxer who has already achieved so much, and such a shame it's against an angry backdrop. Things are being thrown into the ring now, but nobody can wipe the smile off of Cassius Cake's face.

We have witnessed the genesis of something here tonight, folks. The Doughjo is unified for the first time in the two-promotion era. There will be drama in the aftermath, there will be recriminations and accusations, that's for certain. This is an event we will be talking about for years to come, for no doubt a great many different reasons.

But in the ring: a champion has fallen and a new champion has risen.

To the victor: the history. The legacy. The title. The knowledge that there is no-one, not a single boxer out there better than he is over twel- well, thirteen rounds of intense combat.

He is no longer simply the "King".

He is immortal.

He is undeniable.

He is "Undoughsputed" Cassius Cake.

Introducing the Challenger

'I'm going to be the FOOD FiGHT! Champion someday.'

Ring Doughnut's eyes were still glued to the television as a thousand flashing bulbs captured "King" - no, "Undisputed" - Cassius Cake in his moment of ultimate triumph. Seated on the shoulders of his entourage in the middle of a red-roped ring, his blue-and-pink gloves raised in the air on beaten and battered arms, two glorious championship belts draped over each shoulder. Swollen eyes, a cut lip, and an enormous smile despite the torrent of boos.

'Is that so, Ringo?' Granddough replied from his bottle green armchair.

'Yeah. I want to be like Cassius Cake. Is he the best boxer ever?'

'He will be by the time he retires, I'm sure. He's been breaking all sorts of records - and he's still young enough to break a few more before he's done.'

Ring's eyes were still fixed on the screen as Cassius Cake was presented to each side of the arena. Granddough had a newer television, a great big box with a wire antenna, so they'd been able to watch the whole match in colour. It was way better than the television they had at home.

'Was it a good match?' Ring asked.

'Well, I enjoyed it. What did you think?'

'I loved it. It was the best match I've ever seen!'

'It's the only match you've ever seen,' Granddough chuckled, 'but you're not wrong. That was incredible. It had a bit of everything. A shame about the finish.'

'What do you mean?'

'Oh, don't worry. I would've liked a really clean knock-out. Maybe for the "King" to win with his famous "Birthday Bumps". That would've been extra special, wouldn't it?'

'Do you think there will ever be another match as good as that one?' Ring asked. Cassius Cake and his team were finally leaving the ring, a mass of cakes and bakes all funnelling down an aisle between the fans. Some leaned over to try and touch him, others shouted curse words at him. He was next to "Iced" Finger Bun, who seemed to be talking constantly into his ear, his mouth covered.

Granddough laughed once more, creaked out of his chair. He looked just like Ring but older, and with more wrinkles. He wore a pair of thick, plastic spectacles and had granules of sugar stubbled around his face; a slightly unglazed spot on the top of his head that made him look a bit like an egg. Ring felt a hand on his shoulder and was gently ushered him away from the screen. He had been so close he was almost in the ring too.

'Who knows? It would have to really be something, though. The way we never knew who was going to win, and the fact that both the BUN FiGHT! and FOOD FiGHT! Championships were on the line… It's not impossible, but I think we might have started you off with the best match ever, Ringo. How's that for good luck?'

'I'm going to have an even better match when I become champion,' Ring said, followed by a yawn that he stifled. It was very late. Mum never let him stay up this late.

'Oh, is that so? Come on, show me what you've got.' Granddough held out hands in front of him, palms open, fingers pointing towards the ceiling. 'Gently though,' he added.

Ring stood up and turned his back to the television as the main commentator ran through a series of thank yous to the sponsors, the fighters, the support staff, the trainers.

'-and, most importantly, to you, the fans watching at home. Good night.'

The room was dark, illuminated only by the glare of the big screen. A kind of greyish-blue tint to every corner and to Granddough's white vest. A pair of O-shaped shadows thrown onto the wall.

Ring threw a punch with his left hand. His grandfather's right palm cracked a little, but it was soft.

'Good, good. Now try again, but stand a little bit side on. Feet apart - a little more. Great. Go on, same punch,' Granddough said.

With a nod of the head, Ring did as instructed. He must've done something right because Granddough was smiling, dropping in new instructions. He started stepping backwards and moving his hands, and Ring didn't quite catch them but he was close. He clipped Granddough's thumb and heard a noise, a sort of yelp, that he wouldn't have believed his grandfather was capable of.

'Ow, ok, ok. I think you win this round,' Granddough said, pulling him in for a tight hug.

Ring squeezed him back, then wriggled free. He grabbed a soft cushion from the sofa and raised it in the air, parading around the ring.

'Here is your winner and the *new* FOOD FiGHT! Champion: "Prince" Ring Doughnut!' Ring made his voice deeper to do his best impression of the announcer. Granddough clapped loudly and they marched around the room chanting "Prince" with the pillow-title held aloft, Ring waving to the imaginary crowd. He slapped their hands as he left the arena, the corridor acting as his exit aisle.

'Time for bed now, I think. Your mum will not be happy with me when you go back home tired tomorrow.'

'Can't we watch another fight? Or practice some more?'

'Well, Ringo, I think we're going to need to get you a pair of gloves before we go on training. You're too strong! My hands are already sore.'

'Sorry. Can we get some gloves tomorrow? Please.'

'Maybe. I've got to make sure it's ok with your mum first.'

Ring nodded. Mum hated boxing. He'd heard her say as much when Granddough had suggested watching the show together last week. He didn't want to look sad, though, so he gave his biggest, bravest smile.

Granddough must have noticed, 'Don't worry.

She'll come around. Now, off and get ready for bed. I'll come in and say good night.'

Ring hadn't slept a wink.

Granddough's bed was huge and smelled a bit old, and the thick blanket felt heavy on his chest, and the pillows were too hard. The room wasn't as dark as his room at home, and he heard people singing and cheering into the night, seemingly right outside the window. And Granddough was snoring from his chair in the front room, the television still on but just quiet enough that Ring couldn't make out what anyone was saying.

Ring couldn't stop thinking about the fight. About how cool Cassius Cake looked, and how good he was at boxing. About what he'd wear to his matches, who he'd have in his corner. Obviously Granddough. His best friend, Jam Tart. Maybe his sister, Sugar, if she started being a bit nicer to him. Probably some other people he didn't know yet too. Cassius Cake might even join him once Ring had beaten him.

Ring yawned, but he couldn't help but play out that match in his head.

Welcome to the Bread Bin for another amazing night of FOOD FiGHT! action, he thought in the voice of the lead commentator. *In the blue corner, the challenger, "Prince" Ring*

Doughnut. In the red corner, the champion, "King" Cassius Cake.

He rolled around in the bed and he even punching the air a couple of times too. He got knocked over several times by Cassius Cake but he kept getting up with a grumble and a groan and a grunt of effort, and then he had the champion on the ropes. He was about to throw his best punch when there was a gentle knock at the door.

'Ringo, everything ok?' Granddough asked, yawning. He looked really tired; his eyes sunken into his face. 'I thought I heard you.'

'Sorry Granddough,' Ring whispered, 'I'm fine. Just playing.'

'It's a bit late to be playing. Try and get some sleep, ok?'

'I will,' Ring lied. 'Wait, Granddough. Can I ask you something?'

'You just did.' A hushed laugh. 'Go ahead.'

'Do you really think I can be champion?'

'Absolutely, Ringo. Absolutely. You can do anything you put your mind to, and if that's being the best boxer ever then I wouldn't bet against you.'

'Did you ever want to be a boxer?'

'Ah, well. You might not believe me, but I was one, once upon a time.'

'No way!' Ring shouted, and Granddough raised a finger to his mouth. 'Sorry. Sorry. Were you good? Did you win a championship?' Ring continued, this time in a whisper.

'I was quite handy, yes. It was a different time. A long time ago. Not everyone could box professionally. Anyway, that's a much bigger story. I'll tell you some more tomorrow, ok?'

'Ok,' Ring agreed. 'Wait, actually. One more question. Please?'

Granddough sighed playfully. Nodded. 'One more then you have to go to sleep. Deal?' His eyes were bright behind his spectacles and he seemed taller to Ring now.

'Who would win in a match between you and Cassius Cake?'

'Funny you should ask that, Ringo: he's actually the one that retired me.'

Twelve Years Later

'-and, most importantly, to you, the fans watching at home. Good night.'

Ring Doughnut held the television remote up to his mouth like a microphone, mimicked the nasally voice of Walter Waffle. He'd done this all night. Watching the fight, rewinding it, watching it again.

You should have known this was going to happen, he thought, a great big yawn filling the room as he began to rewind the tape again, accompanied by the whirring of the video player.

Ring maintained that the logic had been sound. He needed a good night's sleep ahead of today and he needed to avoid over-thinking or over-imagining what might happen, so having something familiar on in the background would be the right amount of comforting for him to drift off into a deep sleep - and what could be more familiar than "Undoughsputed", the most famous boxing event of all time? Ring had watched it so many times he knew when each and every punch was going to land, so he'd have no issues nodding off.

How wrong he was.

He'd spent the first watch through captivated, sitting up in bed, all the lights on. Not even under his blanket. No effort was made to fall asleep and Ring was willing to admit that he sort of knew that would happen anyway. When Walter Waffle wished him a pleasant evening, he was surprised by the time - but it wasn't unreasonable.

The second time around, he'd laid down, lights out. Straining a little to see the small television screen from his position, occasionally closing his eyes or rolling over to face the other wall only to be bolted back to life when one of the two titans captured the crowd's attention with a flashy combo. He kept waiting for the moment his eyes would become heavy and his blinks would become longer, but the more the battle went on, the more awake he became. Walter Waffle should've been saying good morning to him at the conclusion of the match.

Admittedly, Ring didn't know why he

persisted with his flawed plan for a third time, except that he was now feeling anxious about the lack of sleep. Over-thinking how it may affect him. The tape was no longer playing to lull him to sleep but to distract him from those thoughts, and he found himself watching it even more intently. He kept a scorecard in his head and, as always, he still came out with Cassius Cake winning on points by two rounds - without even counting the thirteenth round.

He probably could've watched it a fourth time but Walter Waffle's farewells now doubled up as an alarm clock. There was no more time for sleep. He had to get up, get ready, and get over to the other side of the Doughjo.

'It's fine, you were studying,' he reassured himself, stifling another yawn.

Today wasn't a good day to be tired. Today was a day of utmost importance, a day where he'd need to be sharp, alert, responsive. Driven and determined and perceptive. The exact opposite of who he was right now as he yawned again, stretched out for what felt like a lifetime. Achey, heavy limbs. What did that mean? Was it a sign?

Focus, he told himself, a one-word mantra boxed into him by Granddough over the years to combat the times when his inquisitive imagination was more of a hindrance than a help.

The video finally stopped rewinding, the mechanism squeaking to a halt. His finger hovered over the play button out of habit.

'No time for that,' he told himself as he turned the television off. 'Today's the biggest day of your life, Ring. The start of your new life. It's time to get up and seize it.'

If only he could get out of bed.

The thin, green-and-white foil wrapper across his chest may as well have been made from stainless steel. His body tingled nervously, from the tips of his toes to the big hole in his centre. His glaze was impressive, darkening the natural brown of his crisp body, giving him a hardened exterior that belied his soft, airy body beneath. That glaze had been hours of work last night, applying and re-applying. Sure, it was a lot of effort, but he wanted to make an impact. He needed to.

After all, that's what the "King" had done. For the first two minutes of his debut bout, the only action was Cassius Cake - then known as "Birthday" - ducking, weaving, bobbing. Untouchable. His opponent wasn't anything special, wasn't anybody who became a somebody, but he was a professional with eight fights and just one loss at the time, and he couldn't lay a glove on the one-day undisputed champion. Then, in the final minute of the round, Cake started punching back - catching his opponent with ease, hitting every single shot. No wasted movement. He nailed a straight right, left hook combination and the opponent crumpled and stayed down. The referee didn't even need to count. A first-round knock-out. The perfect way to arrive on the scene.

Ring Doughnut would like to do that today. He thought the parallel would be quite nice for historians and journalists and commentators to draw in the future, when he was champion.

Shutting his eyes, Ring was no longer in bed, staring at a beige cardboard ceiling.

No, now he was sitting down in an obscenely comfortable chair opposite Walter Waffle to do a pre-fight interview. Laughing like a pair of old friends as they discussed the highs and lows of his career so far, how he'd fought to claim his place at the very top of the roster to challenge the "King", discussing the folks that had made it possible for him to be here.

Quickly on to fight night and he saw his entrance, heard the fans. Acknowledged them, too, with fist bumps and smiles and exchanging a word of wisdom or two. Even though everyone loved Cassius Cake, they'd still be cheering for Ring Doughnut, such was his own popularity. Mostly because they could see his heart, his desire, his love of the sport in each of his excellent performances that propelled him to the main event. To the bout that would change his life.

Suddenly, he was in the ring, in the final round of the match. Looming large in the other corner: "King" Cassius Cake.

A moment he'd played out so often in his mind, the scene was so clear it was more of a premonition than a memory. Cassius Cake appeared in silhouette with the lights bright behind him, showcasing his extraordinary frame and size. Though technically a cupcake, the "King" was somewhere between a muffin and a cake in size and weight. His light blue case acted as a mask, the thin, light-blue paper helping to keep his real identity hidden but not his enormous grin; and a swirl of pink buttercream icing was quaffed neatly on his head.

'Across the ring from the reigning champion is the wildcard. Unbeaten in all his fights as a professional, winning all of them by knock-out,' Ring said to himself, eyes closed, visualising the scene at the Cake Stand Stadium where all the biggest fights were held in Calorifornia. Ever since he could remember, he'd commentate on his own made-up matches. For the play-by-play, it had to be the legendary, iconic voice of Walter Waffle, heralded for his rapid-fire delivery and straight-down-the-middle commentary.

'A certain underdog, but the one they call "Prince", the icing-covered warrior from the sweet side of the bakery, is holding his own here against the very best to have ever set foot in the ring. We're into the final few rounds and Doughnut will need to find something special.'

'Special? He wouldn't know special if it hit him in the face - and it is right now!' This voice wasn't based on anyone, but rather a collection of contrarian commentators that Ring had listened to over the years, and was known as Bazz.

(Ring had a whole backstory for Bazz. A ball doughnut who had a bright future before suffering a career-ending injury to Ring Doughnut, Bazz moved into punditry and analysis with the expressed purpose of watching his old rival's downfall from a front row seat.)

Ring rolled out of bed and started shadow boxing, pawing a jab towards the spectre of the greatest fighter in history. He dodged one of Cake's famous jabs himself, drawing *oos* and *ahs* from the crowd who were impressed with his agility even into the dying rounds of the fight.

'Doughnut's a student of the game and he knows he needs to throw Cake off of the script, needs to sew some doubt in there or something,' he said, this time in a familiar, thicker accent that made him smile. 'If anyone can do it, it's my grandson. Go get 'em, Ringo!' Granddough was not known for being unbiased in these shadow-spars and he loved to wind Bazz up. Even against Cassius Cake, Ring was pretty sure his grandfather would be rooting for him.

'Both fighters are toiling out there but Cassius Cake is locked in. This is normally the time he tries to finish a match with his signature move,' Waffle continued.

Ring threw another punch, but of course the illusion of Cassius Cake dodged it, blocked the follow up, clobbered Ring with an expert straight shot of his own. Ring came in for the clinch to buy himself some time.

'Hang in there, Ringo!' Granddough encouraged.

'He's got nothing left. He should throw in the towel already!' Bazz added.

'What heart, what effort from the young challenger,' Waffle interrupted, 'he just needs to hold on, weather the storm. All he needs is one good punch to change his life.'

They broke and Ring was on the back foot again, pressed up against the cardboard wall of his room, between the standing punchbag with its taped-up holes and a poster of the man he was facing.

Cassius Cake launched a series of stinging punches to the mid-section. A standard precursor to his signature and, even though Ring knew that, he couldn't stop them such was their sheer force.

'We all know what comes next, folks,' Waffle warned.

'The end. At long last.'

Cassius Cake rocked back on his heels and then fired a salvo of punches, blistering quick to Ring's arms and shoulders. Rapid-fire hooks fired from a wide, swaying position that numbed him. Ring's guard couldn't hold, and suddenly he was wide open. *Boom!* Two fists sandwiched his chin.

Ring crashed to the floor at the base of his bed. Eyes closed, breathing heavy.

'The crowd are on their feet, it's all over. It's all over. Nobody has ever beat the ten count after being hit by Cake's ultimate finishing manoeuvre, the "Birthday Bumps"!' Waffle reminded him.

Ring, now referee as well, called out the numbers.

'6, 7-'

'I don't believe it, he's getting back up! Can he beat the count?'

'Go on, Ringo! You can do it!'

'-8, 9-'

'No way!'

'He's up, he's back to his feet. He's survived the

"Birthday Bumps" and even Cassius Cake is smiling. Nobody has ever got up from that. History is made here!' Waffle shouted (or would have done, except Ring didn't want to wake up the neighbours; instead, it came out as a ferocious whisper).

Ring, rejuvenated, was back on the offensive and Cake couldn't touch him. He was focused, he landed alternating punches to the mid-section - the punchbag rattling with each one, a little more stuffing puffing out - and he could see that Cassius Cake was almost down now.

'He's going for a finishing move of his own. Could it be? Yes! He hits the "Glazed Over"-', an uppercut with a wide, low starting position and a high-power follow-through, '-and the champion is down! Cassius Cake is down!'

Ring Doughnut counted out the numbers, standing respectfully over his opponent and interrupted occasionally by Bazz in disbelief, knowing full well he wouldn't get back up. The referee reached ten and then he celebrated, running around his room, arms raised, pointing to the crowd. He checked on the fallen champion who shook his hand and acknowledged him, raised his arm as well.

'Here is your winner and the *new* undisputed FOOD FiGHT! Champion: "Prince" Ring

Doughnut!'

Ring raised his arms aloft, stood on his bed, basking in the adulation of the crowd. He rattled off statistics in his head: second youngest winner, first person to ever beat Cassius Cake, first new champion in over a decade, the lineal champion of BUN FiGHT! as well (even if the promotion would refuse to recognise him), first doughnut, first fighter from Alacrumba.

He ran to hug his grandfather at ringside, to acknowledge the part he had played in all of this. Arms raised again.

Ring looked at the posters of the great fighters that adorned his bedroom wall. The names, the faces, the moments. Not all champions but all great enough to have been immortalised in print.

He couldn't wait to join them.

Successfully out of bed, Ring Doughnut chucked his gear into a blue shoulder bag. He'd packed it the night before but, wracked by a nagging feeling he had forgotten something, he had emptied it and was now meticulously announcing each item as they were re-added into the leather hold-all.

'Right glove, left glove. Pink icing. Spare pads. Spare shorts. Tape.' He looked around his immediate vicinity to see if he'd missed anything. 'Towel,' he said, folding up the small white rectangle and adding it to the mix. That hadn't made it first time.

See, he told himself, *this wasn't stupid after all.*

Ring had only recently moved out of the family home to a top shelf apartment of his own. On days like today, where he was up early and needed to focus, he was glad for the quiet - but it would've been nice to hear his mum wish him good luck, to be taunted by his older sister. He was sure that was her way of encouraging him. Or that's what he liked to think, anyway.

His lounge was pretty empty, a sofa made from an old milk carton that had seen better days; the floor still bare, exposed cardboard the same colour as the ceiling. He tended to spend his tokens on his gear, training equipment, the odd bit of memorabilia. The only time his mum had visited she'd commented on his need to get a few more bits and pieces to make the place more *him.*

So he took her advice. Propped up opposite his sofa, a framed FOOD FiGHT! Championship belt. A replica of the exact one that the Cassius Cake carried to the ring every single match.

That'll be the real thing one day, he smiled, staring at the shiny gold plates on the black leather.

Alongside the belt was a dull grey tin can on a white string, and he suddenly realised he'd almost forgotten to call Jam - which would surely mean his best friend would have also forgotten and would still be sound asleep. He picked up the can and, after a couple of moments, he asked to be connected to the Tart residence. The gentle, rhythmic tugging of the can signalled that nobody had answered. Then again, it was quite early.

Just as he was about to hang up, Ring heard a voice on the other end of the line. Snappy.

'Colonel Custard here. Who's calling at this time? Over.'

'Hello, sir. It's Ring Doughnut, calling for Jam. I'm really sorry it's so early but I wanted to make sure he's ready, as I'll be leaving soon. Sorry again, I didn't mean to wake you. Over.' Ring always got nervous talking to Jam's grandfather. Colonel Custard Tart could be kind and warm and generous; or he could be strict, sharp, and short-tempered. Ring had not yet understood the consistency of those moods.

'Ah, young master Doughnut. Jam told me about today. Good luck. Your grandfather would be so proud.' The Colonel's tone had mellow quickly. 'If he isn't awake yet, I'll be sure to get him out of bed without hesitation. He'll be outside the house awaiting your arrival. Over.'

'Thank you, sir. I appreciate it. Sorry again. Over and out.'

Ring was glad that Colonel Custard had

answered the call. Jam would've just said he was awake and fallen back to sleep not a minute later. At least with the Colonel bellowing orders and marching Jam around, he'd have a chance of getting out on time.

After a quick scan of each room – all now in a state of dishevelment – Ring knew he had to get going. What he hadn't packed wouldn't affect him and he didn't want to delay himself any more. Besides, getting out into some fresh air would help calm his nerves.

This is it, he thought. *This is the day.*

He pushed open the door and took his first step.

Ring's apartment was on the bottom of a three-box building on the top shelf. The aisle-facing facade was a mismatch of three or four different boxes, all held together with bright yellow tape. Coarsely cut square-ish holes were filled by transparent plastic sheets that acted as windows. They let in a little fluorescent light and, if he was awake late enough, Ring Doughnut could sometimes catch some of the sunset from the world outside of the Doughjo.

One of the perks of living way up in Alacrumba heights.

Maybe the only perk, actually.

It took ages to get anywhere as every journey

began with the descent to the shop floor via four cold sets of stairs and, even if he did get a good deal because his mum knew his landlord, he was still paying premium rent. Still, Ring enjoyed having his own space. Somewhere to discover himself, to follow his path.

Besides, he wouldn't be here long once his boxing career took off.

Just outside his front door, he noted how quiet the bakery was in the early morning. He looked down at the empty solid wood floors and across to the other sections: a cluster of dark wooden tables and shelves; glass display cases and fancy stands; poorly lit corners, made dimmer by the lavishness of the great, wide window, empty except for the words 'The Doughjo' written in reverse in beautiful gold stencil.

Straight beneath the bold text and bathed in the warmth of the morning sun, the shop window was home to the rich and glamorous folks of Calorifornia. A haven for celebrities and the nondescript schmoozers who always seemed to find a way into that world. The window display was an elaborate layout of clear, free-standing shelves, all of which were filled with exquisite homes twice the size of the building that Ring lived in, with less than half the amount of people. Just beneath the window itself, the hotels on the shop floor were exquisite pieces, designed by the very best architects in the Doughjo.

Ring planned to buy his first house there, and find one big enough that he'd even let his mum and sister stay - the latter on the condition that she admit his hobby wasn't so stupid after all.

There used to be a lot of gyms and smaller arenas, although that space had been gobbled up by the need for more outrageous properties. To consolidate, the existing Cake Stand Stadium was scheduled to be knocked down and replaced with an even bigger version that would act as a sports hub for generations of Calorifornians to come.

To the left and next to the door, was Breadinburgh. Of all the poorly lit corners, that was the worst. The old, thick shelves sagged down from the wall, hanging over wicker baskets and a small table that wobbled. The fabled Bread Bin, the birthplace of boxing, had long since lost its lustre, the light oak box now lacquered in thick black paint. Inside, it was apparently falling to disrepair - though Breadinburgh had long since stopped allowing guests from the rest of the bakery to travel there.

All because of a fight, Ring scoffed. He didn't see why there was such a controversy around the result. It was obvious Cassius Cake had won. If anything, the fans should've been happy to see an extra round.

Still, the fallout from that fight and BUN FiGHT!'s subsequent refusal to acknowledge the result - and, thus, acknowledge Cassius Cake's undisputed status - had led to tensions, particularly between Breadinburgh and Calorifornia. The acrimony had got so bad that the space between them, where the door would swing open to the tune of a little brass bell, was simply abandoned. A buffer between two worlds. The Deserted Aisle.

On the other side of the sloping shelves of Breadinburgh, the grey door to the kitchen isolated them further from the rest of the Doughjo. Ring had never been to the kitchen, but his mum had once, and she described it as a strange place where both 'the best and worst minds' in the bakery resided. They didn't have any interest in boxing either, so Ring never really thought about what was beyond that porthole window - aside from what the people of New Yolk and Flourida did for fun if not the pursuit of pugilism.

A glass display unit, known as Chillinois, home to the coolest desserts and traybakes, stood proudly, illuminated in a faded, blue light almost all the time. Frank Chouxno had started on his journey here, with their style of boxing marked by precision and consistency. The rings were impressive too, with the jewel in the crown being the Pedestal, a giant crystal display stand in the centre of Chillinois that put on open-air bouts. That arena was towards the top of Ring's wish list to compete in.

The Alacrumba district was in the back corner of the bakery, and that was where Ring lived alongside other doughnuts, cookies, and assorted goods. A jolly place and a fairly relaxed setting, it felt totally un-noteworthy to Ring. It was just home, a comforting blandness. (Ring's mum hated when he described it in this way.) He could count back the generations of Doughnuts who had lived here, and he found that both immensely reassuring and utterly terrifying.

Next to them was Mississipie, a hostile place that was trying to become a little bit less terrifying and hostile by adding some colour to an otherwise exclusively brown and grey set of buildings. It did smell fantastic though. A perfect alliance of hot fruit and warm pastry wafting over on conditioned air from the clanking machine that loomed over their shelves.

To the right of that was Bisconsin, also known as the Central Biscuit District, home to many biscuits who scurried around in suits talking in acronyms and initialisations about stocks and tokens, as if any of it really mattered, moving from one gigantic foil-faced building to another. Ring's mum's friend's daughter worked there, and she was making a lot of tokens at the sacrifice of getting any sleep at all. Ring didn't think that was a good deal. Then again, he imagined his mum's friend's daughter probably didn't think getting punched in the face for tokens was a good deal, either.

Ring took a deep breath, inhaled the scents of the Doughjo. The sights, the sounds. He wanted to remember this time before everything changed for him. He wouldn't always be able to enjoy these moments of peacefulness, of stillness. Not when he was champion.

'Alright, let's go,' he said, and he taped his door down in place. The flap of cardboard was rigid and thick and always caught on the black wire frames of the shelf beneath. It took a couple of sticks to get it to stay in place. He'd have to talk to the landlord about that.

A job for tomorrow, he told himself. He'd need to stay focused.

He heaved his bag onto his shoulder, reminded himself of what lay ahead.

The opportunity of a lifetime.

Ring checked his bag one final time and, satisfied, he walked over to the stairway that led to the shelves below and, ultimately, to the first day of his new life.

'You didn't have to call my gramps up, you know?' Jam Tart said, jumping up from the front step of his house. A grand old mansion, it was faded yellow cardboard and four floors, occupied on a permanent basis by Jam Tart and his grandfather, and occasionally by a variety of relatives who seemed to show up when they had nowhere else to go.

'So you were awake?' Ring grinned.

'Well-'

'-That's a 'no', then-'

'-I was having a tactical power nap. You know, make sure I've got enough energy for the big day.'

Ring laughed and continued on the descent to the shop floor. The early start meant the stairs were quiet, and their footsteps seemed to echo all the way up to the top of the bakery off of the cold metal.

'You should've heard him, my gramps,' Jam continued, 'I think he likes you more than he likes me. Kept going on about how I couldn't let you down, how I had to get up, get ready. How it's a very important day for you. I swear, if I'd messed up by even a minute, I'd have pushed him a day closer to his expiry date.'

'I'll have to thank him.'

'Just get him some ringside tickets for your championship fight.' Jam nudged Ring in the side with his elbow, made a *heh* sound.

Ring thought about how long he'd known Jam Tart. They went way back, as far back as anyone Ring had known that wasn't related to him, and it seemed to him that Jam had never changed. Not least because he was still quite short compared to Ring, who wasn't tall himself. They'd got on immediately and been firm friends ever since, with Jam's easy-breeziness proving a perfect foil to Ring's more studious, rigid nature. Even if Jam didn't seem to have any direction to his life at the moment, he was always Ring's number one supporter, always hyping him up. Jam had never once doubted that Ring would make it as a boxer. As *the* boxer.

'Deal.'

Of course, Ring had always supported Jam, too - though the list of pursuits there was considerably longer and more varied. Writer, poet, musician, artist, presenter, writer again, (briefly) boxer, manager, coach, and (currently) journalist. That's why he was coming along today: Jam was going to write up Ring's entire journey, from the very first day to the day he held the belt above his head.

(Ring had reminded him that today wasn't the *first* day, but was actually the culmination of his determination and perseverance throughout his entire life so far. Jam had replied that he would cover those bits in the autobiography, or at least in a retrospective article.)

'So, how are you feeling today?' Jam asked, holding a notepad and pencil. From his satchel bag, he'd pulled out an old grey trilby with a little square of white paper tucked into the black band that wrapped around it and perched it on his shortcrust head. It had the word 'PRESS' written on it, and looked out of place against his shiny red face.

'Erm.' Ring paused. *How* am *I feeling?* 'Excited, mostly.'

'Mmhmm.'

Ring looked at Jam, who circled his hands around each other.

'Yeah. I guess just excited, really.'

'Any nerves?' Jam asked.

Yes. 'No, not really. I feel pretty good about the whole thing.'

'Why?'

'What do you mean?'

'Why aren't you nervous? You're about to have a try out at the Sponge Dungeon, the elite development gym which produced legendary fighters such as "Drop-dead" Fred Velvet, Garrotte Cake, and, the most famous of them all-'

'-"King" Cassius Cake,' Ring finished. 'I know, I know who's passed through there. And I know it's run by Victor Sponge, before you say anything.

And I know what he's achieved, too, so you can save your breath on that one.'

'You're impressed, though, right? I did do some background research,' Jam smiled, feigned doffing his hat. 'Anyway. Back to my question. What makes you think you've got what it takes to succeed here?'

Ring chewed on the inside of his mouth. He just sort of *knew* he was good enough, but that wouldn't make sense. Might sound a bit arrogant, as well, and he wanted to make sure he came across as humble if this article ever did see the light of day. Cassius Cake always seemed so grounded, so likeable. That's what Ring wanted for his career, too.

'It's… my… destiny,' Ring said, the words sort of falling out against his will. He realised he had missed the mark on humble when Jam sniggered, muttered something under his breath. 'No, that's not what I meant. Not like that. Look, can we maybe not do the interview right now, Jam? Have you got everything you need? I want to focus.'

They reached the bottom of the stairs and hit the shop floor, greeted by the smell of butter and sawdust, and the sight of hotels and shops which were barely blinking into life. Little blue lights appearing in the plastic windows up and down the aisle.

'One last question. No, please. Just one.'

Ring sighed. Nodded.

'What's your motivation, Mr Doughnut? Why pursue a career in something so competitive and so physically demanding? What gets you out of bed on a morning like today to follow this path?'

He walked forward a few more steps on the wooden floor, past the bright facades of his home town. There weren't many folks up and about at this time, and those who were shuffled groggily, aimlessly. He wondered if any would be heading to the Sponge Dungeon. The thought made him uneasy.

I don't want to have to fight someone I know.

'Ring? I promise it's the last question,' Jam nudged softly.

'Oh, sorry. Yeah, my... motivation.' Ring looked up to the fluorescent lights as they began to flicker into life. Of the three directly above them, two buzzed and hummed, casting their yellow haze down across the shelves they'd just descended from. One, though, flickered and blinked, made a gentle *clink* sound as it desperately tried to stay on. 'It's all I've ever wanted to do, really. From the first time I watched a match, I knew this was the path for me. Is that a good enough answer?'

Jam screwed up his face a little. 'I guess, but like... Yeah, I guess.'

Ring mentally sighed.

'Ok, so: my grandfather got me into boxing when I was younger. He was actually a boxer too, back in the day. If FOOD FiGHT! had come around a bit sooner, he might've been a champion there. Anyway, he trained me and he always said I was good enough to be the champ, so I want to prove him right. I want to add the Doughnut name to the hall of fame.'

'Fair point, good point. I like that it rhymes. The granddad angle is great too, that'll pull on the emotions. I'm writing it down.'

Ring felt a bit uncomfortable. It was too personal. Like he'd exposed a piece of his soul to everyone. Then again, it also felt stilted and generic. What did Jam mean by 'the granddad angle', anyway? Whenever Cassius Cake spoke it was so eloquent and engaging, and Ring couldn't help but feel he'd offered a whole lot of nothing.

Jam took off his trilby and put it back in the bag along with the notepad and pencil. 'Ok, so, no more questions until we get there - but I am not walking all the way to Calorifornia in silence.'

'Fine, what do you want to talk about?' Ring asked.

'What's up with you and Angel? She said-'

'-Nope, not talking about her today, either. Something else.'

'Ok, ok. Duly noted. Erm… You see they're turning that book into a TV show?'

'Which book?'

'The one with the murders and they don't know who's done them. By whatshername.'

'I have literally no idea what you're talking about.'

'She's, like, mega-famous. She does murder mysteries and stuff like that.'

'And yet you can't remember her name?' Ring laughed.

'It's still early, ok!' Jam responded cheerfully. 'Did you see the stuff about Cassius Cake's retirement? Apparently the next fight is going to be his last.'

Ring doubted that very much. Rumours of Cake's retirement had been going into overdrive this year. Some fans were saying he'd get out before he got beat; others were saying he wouldn't stop until he'd been beaten. Some suspected he would retire because he wasn't as good as he once was; others pointed out that he had won almost all of his recent fights by knock-out or unanimous decision.

As the champion's biggest fan, Ring Doughnut had spent time pondering this very question; as the boxer who was destined to dethrone him, he already knew the answer.

'Oh really? He hasn't even announced an opponent yet, or when it'll be,' Ring replied.

'Yeah, he said something in the press conference after Undoughsputed about retiring after a dozen years and the maths adds up.'

'Ha! Everyone is still falling for that? He's said loads of stuff over the years that he's then walked back on. He isn't retiring soon.'

'I don't know, mate. When I read about it, it did sound pretty convincing.'

'They always do. I'd be willing to bet he'll still be here next year. There's nobody on his level, anyway.' *Yet.*

'That's true,' Jam agreed. 'Well, anyway. How's your mum? How's your sister?'

Ring rolled his eyes. 'Mum's fine, thanks. Not even going to bother with the sister comment.'

'Have you put in a good word for me?' Jam *heh*'d.

'Oh my- Jam, I'd rather you went back to interviewing me.'

'What? Can't a friend innocently ask about his friend's family?'

'I'm putting my headphones on now.'

'You know, that's very ru...'

From his bag, Ring pulled out a cassette player and a pair of ugly but comfortable headphones. It was a gift from his mum when he moved out to help 'fill the silence'. He'd imagined she would want him to listen to storybooks or business lectures on the device, but Ring had other ideas. The rest of Jam's protest was safely drowned out by the inimitable sound of Dave Gruel and the rest of the Chew Fighters, and Ring Doughnut couldn't help but let their epic guitar riffs and raw vocals provide the soundtrack to his imagination of what was to come on this momentous day.

Round 3:
Starter

Calorifornia hadn't always been in the window and characterised by massive mansions, decadent displays, and fantastical frontages.

Apparently, according to Old Linzer Torte, who had been around longer than anybody else Ring knew, this area of the bakery used to be called Bunchester, and had been full of breads and baps and rolls and other sorts who now lived in Breadinburgh.

Calorifornia actually originated on a nearby table set between Bunchester and Bisconsin (which had also formerly been a bread-based area known as Loafdon). The round, dark reddish table had been home to just a few simple cakes to begin with, but within a few years it had expanded rapidly with a variety of different colours and lavish displays, and it sprawled into areas of Bunchester, quickly claiming the entire window and developing the suburbs beneath it too.

Most cakes didn't want to live in 'Old Calorifornia' any more, given the slight isolation and awkward transport links, and the nearby glitz and glamour of the new home. Falling into slight disrepair, the area was saved by its most famous son, the iconic, almost mythical Victor Sponge, who saw that the isolation would be the perfect place for the most focused, determined boxers to hone their craft.

It was at the base of this table, the dark red faded, that Ring and Jam stood today, surrounded by others who all had the same destination in mind: the two matte black, cold, circular tins perched in the middle of the tabletop. The Sponge Dungeon. This was the place responsible for many of the most impressive boxing careers that had ever been. Pretty much all of the greats had spent some time here. It was a place of history and heritage; of legacy and learning; imagination and innovation.

It was a place that Ring Doughnut hoped to soon call home.

'Long way up,' Jam noted, staring towards the tabletop. 'Can't see any stairs, either.'

Ring looked around and he couldn't see an easy

route up there either. Couldn't even see the Sponge Dungeon itself any more, just the dusty, dark underside of the table, a stark contrast to the hot sun that was pouring in, warming the wood beneath their feet. Ring was glad he hadn't already applied his icing, as it would have been dripping down his face and body by now. He squinted against the thick rays.

'Maybe we have to go into New Calorifornia?' He suggested.

'Why don't we just ask someone?' Jam offered.

'No, it's fine.'

Ring didn't want to be struggling already, not before he'd even got there. Didn't want to owe anyone anything before he'd thrown a punch.

Jam had no such issues, and he started over towards a small, sugary biscuit who was carrying a pair of blue gloves, not dissimilar to Ring's. After what seemed an animated chat, Jam signalled to him.

'Janice says there's a lift, if we want to walk with her?'

'It's fine, we can make our own way,' Ring replied quietly.

'Mate, come on,' Jam nudged him, smiled.

'It's just-'

'-Just nothing. I'll go with Janice, then, and if you happen to follow me, so be it? Deal?'

Ring said nothing and followed his friend over to whoever this Janice was.

'I couldn't believe they accepted my application. I'm so excited. *Eeee!*'

Janice had rivalled Jam for how much she could talk - and she spoke at such speed that Ring could barely keep up in the conversation. Jam, however, seemed to be in his element. He *heh*'d and rallied back and forth with her, a permanent grin on his shiny red face.

So far, Ring had ascertained that Janice had applied for the trial day, just as he had. A written application with a short video skills package, showing some basic punches and stances, answering some standard questions around suitability, commitment, community outreach, etcetera, etcetera. Nothing outstanding there.

Janice was two years older than them and seen her application to join the Sponge Dungeon rejected twice before.

'They say you don't get more than one chance to impress here so I really need to nail this one today,' she giggled.

Further proof that this is my destiny, Ring reminded himself, knowing that he'd sent off one application as soon as he was old enough - and been accepted immediately. He had assumed that marked him as special, particularly as his research indicated that the chances of a first-time, just-old-enough applicant getting a trial were basically non-existent.

Prospective trainees could apply as many times as they liked, but once they'd had a trial, they couldn't apply again - although they could be invited back. Realistically, though, nobody ever got a second chance. Ring knew that, which is why he was spending his time in line for the elevator running through drills in his head, calling out patterns as he had done many times before in his room, and not aimlessly chatting about the heat and the colour of the table cloth.

The elevator was a rickety-looking contraption, not really befitting of the Sponge Dungeon. Or maybe it was the first test. Bravery. Courage.

An old egg box without a lid carried half a dozen would-be boxers up to the tabletop, attached by a couple of pieces of string that looked exactly like the type used to connect the tin cans between houses. It wobbled and rocked, jerkily hoisting the next six up and above and towards their moment of truth.

'We should be in the next one. How exciting,' Janice said, looking at both of them expectantly, 'I've always wanted to try out one of these egg-pulley lifts.'

'Surely they could have just built some stairs?' Jam suggested.

'No way. No. What? No. The old town is made special by things like this. It's quaint. I like it,' Janice replied.

'Oh, no. Yeah, no. Me too. I love it,' Jam said. 'I meant, like, they could've built some stairs but that would be out of character. This is much better. Unique. Isn't it, Ring?'

'It's slow,' Ring said.

He was eager to get started now. To land his first punch, to complete his first set. He knew that he'd work hard today and standing in the hot, hazy sunlight wasn't the ideal preparation. He'd seen about three loads go up, so did that mean there were going to be twenty of them? More? And how early had they all got up to get here before him? It was already mid-morning and they would've been here much later if it wasn't for Jam flagging down a passing milk cart, the driver of which was happy to drop them off on the edge of Bisconsin. Ring hadn't caught her name, but he was sure Jam had, given he scribbled down almost everything she said in his notebook (though, mercifully, he didn't wear the hat).

'Oh, seems like someone's a bit nervous,' Janice smiled, her voice light and sweet.

Jam jumped in before Ring could bite back, limiting the blast radius. 'My mate? No way, Ring Doughnut does not get nervous. He's zoned in. Focused. When he's in fight mode, he's like a different person.' Jam stopped, obviously felt the pressure to add more as the silence landed uncomfortably. 'That's why he's being a bit short.'

'Yeah. Just how I get into the zone,' Ring added.

'I get it, I have a routine too. The opposite to you though - I get louder when I'm nervous, just want to drown out the over-thinking. You know?' Janice kept nodding her head, and Ring nodded back for some reason. 'Yeah. It's funny, how we're all trying to do the same thing but in different ways.'

The egg box was coming back down. Quicker than it went up, at least.

Jam and Janice kept talking, and Ring drifted in and out of the conversation, noticing that his best friend was repeating some of the questions he'd asked Ring earlier. Janice seemed nice, sweet. Her background was in sprinting, actually, but she had always enjoyed watching boxing with her brothers and sisters, and felt she had the agility to be quite handy between the ropes.

(Ring was suspicious at this point. He couldn't believe that Victor Sponge would have accepted her with that background alone. Either she was lying to Jam, or something had gone wrong with the candidates this year. The Sponge Dungeon only took on the very best bakes - so why extend the invitation to someone who just happened to 'like boxing'?)

The egg box landed softly on the wood floor ahead of them.

One by one, six dejected faces exited. A pair of gloves in one hand, a bag over a shoulder. Red eyes, gritted teeth. A swollen cheek or two.

'What happened up there?' Jam wondered out loud.

A blueberry muffin with thick arms and legs and a towering frame flashed his eyes up at him, opened his mouth, then shook his head, his thoughts lost somewhere between them. Behind him, a bourbon biscuit covered in old cuts and scars simply dragged his thumb across his body and made a snapping sound, a grin on his face but sadness in his eyes.

They didn't make it, Ring thought. Not that he was surprised, or shocked. Or even sad. There would be plenty who wouldn't make it today, given that the Sponge Dungeon only ever took on a single rookie each year.

What had surprised him though is how early the rejected applicants had been told to depart the process. Mid-morning. Not even half a day in the hallowed shadow of this most prestigious of gyms. Ring didn't know how long the process would take, but he'd assumed that he would get at least a day to show his skills.

You have to be on it from the first moment you're up there, Ring. No mistakes, he commanded himself. *Don't be like them.*

They lined up for their spots in the egg box lift. A slice of cake went in first, then a fruit scone, followed by Janice, Jam, and Ring. A brownie shuffled awkwardly past Ring to fill up the half dozen.

'It's not nice to see them like that, but it does make me feel better about all of this. If that lot couldn't make it, then there's no shame if I don't either, you know?' Janice said, to which Jam agreed, as they stuttered off the floor and up to the table.

The Sponge Dungeon stood as a matte black beacon to all the would-be boxers in the Doughjo. It was the best gym, with the best boxers, the best coaches, and the most prestige. If you ever wanted to be a champion, your best bet was getting an education here.

Located in the middle of the table, above the single thick wooden leg, it was surrounded by four rings - five black ropes, black aprons, grey mats, red turnbuckle pads - that were each occupied by a trainer and a candidate displaying their skills. Ring had heard their punches even before the egg-lift reached the top of the table: the sound of air wheezing out of pads as they were struck; of punch bags being thumped; the grunting of effort.

Ring quickly scanned the scene to try and pick out Victor Sponge but to no avail. He had hoped to catch a glimpse of the head trainer and former champion. By all accounts, he was an authoritative figure who demanded discipline and hard work, and was quite reclusive. He never did press interviews any more - not since he retired - but he was an accomplished orator and easy company, according to those who knew him.

If Ring was disappointed not to see the head honcho, then it soon gave way to excitement as he noticed the diminutive, bright red figure of "Drop-Dead" Fred Velvet in the ring closest to them. "Drop-Dead" was a rapid, dangerous puncher in his day and was often described as 'the best to have never won the belt' in fan and magazine polls. To be at such close proximity to FOOD FiGHT! royalty… Ring had to rein himself in. He was here on merit, here for a reason. For his destiny. Not as a fan.

Still, though: he's on my wall at home, he

smiled to himself.

'Sign in this way. This way to sign in,' droned a bored, tired-looking cupcake.

Ring followed, along with Jam and Janice - neither of whom had stopped talking on the ride up. Ring had caught a couple of *tsks* from someone behind him, and he had to stop himself from groaning at the incessant noise. He may have also been a tiny, tiny bit jealous.

'Describe to me how you feel in this moment,' Jam said, his hat back on his head.

'Excited, ready to start. I just want to get between the ropes now,' Ring replied. To be honest, he wasn't initially sure the question was directed at him, so he was relieved when Jam scribbled down the response. *Hope he doesn't mix my answers up with hers, though.*

'What does it mean to be this close to your dream?'

'Hard to put into words. It's surreal. It's just… Yeah, surreal.'

'*Heh*, you could try to use more words. Mind if I paraphrase for you a bit on this part?' Jam asked.

'Whatever you need to do.'

'And you, Janice: how do you feel?'

Ring resisted the urge to sigh. It was fine, maybe the comparison between the two would be good. A triumph and a failure. Something like that.

However, Jam was going to angle it, Ring did not fancy being subjected to another one of Janice's rambling monologues, so he quickened his pace towards the sign in area.

The queue at the sign in desk was short and being expertly handled by a team of cupcakes who looked identical to the first one Ring had seen - even in their general demeanour. They handed out numbers and ticked names off of their list with pace.

From his place in the queue, Ring noted the sheer number of participants here today. There must have been dozens of them waiting for their shot at glory, stood around the rings or being held at other cupcake-marshalled checkpoints. It was a lot busier than he had expected when he woke up.

More of them to go home disappointed.

Ring was called over to a cupcake who was wearing a black paper case and had enormous bags under their eyes.

'Name?' He said.

'Ring Doughnut, nice to meet you. And yo-'

'From?'

'Err. From Alacrumba.'

The cupcake scanned down a list, pencil poised between two fingers. Scanned back up the list. Looked at Ring dead in the eyes for a second or two longer than was comfortable.

Ring was about to ask if everything was alright, when the cupcake spoke again.

'Experience?'

'I've done a lot of bag work, loads of gym work. My grandfather trained me and he was a bo-'

'Experience. Fight record. Numbers,' the cupcake interrupted him.

'Oh. Err. Well, no official matches so fa-'

'None,' the cupcake confirmed, now scratching something down in pencil on a piece of white card. 'Number 103. Follow the signs.'

Ring was ushered away with his number now held tightly in his hands. He reminded himself that nothing had gone wrong, even though he felt it had. They were probably just busy, had a lot to get through today. That was all it was. Tired minds doing a repetitive task. Ring knew that all too well from the long days he'd spent at work with his mum and sister, wishing he was elsewhere. Tokens were great and all but, ultimately, that administrator had probably wanted to be a boxer before failing to make the grade and seeing this as the next best thing.

Cut them some slack, he decided.

He turned and looked for Jam, who was stood with Janice while she registered with a different cupcake. She was directed in a separate direction and it seemed to take Jam ages to say goodbye to her, to wish her luck, to say he'd keep in contact, to wish her luck again.

'I almost went without you,' Ring said.

'*Heh*, sorry. She's a nice biscuit. I think you'd like her if you weren't so focused on the day,' he said, before quickly adding, 'not that I blame you for that. Not that there's any blame to go around because nobody's done anything wrong.'

'Don't worry. I know what you're saying,' Ring laughed. That felt good for a moment. But he couldn't ease up. Needed to stay focused.

He followed a conveyor belt of others, directed by a sign that said '100-150 this way'. He did notice a small ball doughnut just ahead but he couldn't work out if he knew them or not, and he didn't want to catch-up to find out. Otherwise, it seemed to be mainly cake-based.

That's good. Easier for me to stand out, he reasoned.

Jam didn't say much as they walked, but he did make admiring noises looking at the rings and the dungeon itself. They went past the ring that "Drop-Dead" Fred Velvet was occupying, and Ring was so close he could see that the once-jet black icing moustache was now whitish, and that the signature red quiff of icing up top was a bit thinner these days. Still, Velvet looked in incredible shape.

Even though the top prize in the sport had eluded him, he did have the prestige of fighting Victor Sponge to a draw (and then losing two further fights in the trilogy) as well as a valiant points loss in his final match against Cassius Cake. Most observers agreed that, in another era, "Drop-Dead" would have been a dominant champion, or at least have won the biggest prize once.

Ring Doughnut wondered if Velvet was happy with his career; wondered if he himself would be happy to have had a similar career when he was ready to hang his gloves up. "Best of the Rest" Ring Doughnut, a fan-favourite who never won anything. Would he be satisfied?

He already knew the answer.

'Any further and we may as well be back home,' Jam joked.

The signs for those given a number between 100 and 150 had continued to point them onwards, circling around the Sponge Dungeon. They'd kept on marching past the rings set up outside, then got so close to the entrance to the dungeon that he thought he might've been chosen to bypass the sparring sessions altogether and step into the hallowed halls - only to be cruelly whisked away towards the back of the building once more.

Still, being that close. It meant something. It

felt right.

They eventually stopped as part of a group of a dozen and a half standing in front of another pair of cupcakes. These two were bigger, quieter. Held heavy builds and wore thick sunglasses, arms crossed over their chests. When a voice through a megaphone shouted 'Next', the cupcakes signalled and allowed a quartet of contenders to enter a rather sparse looking area behind them.

Ring couldn't see any apparatus set up, but he could see a panel of three sat behind a couple of tables. A chocolate cake, a lemon muffin, and a thick slice of fruit cake that was so densely populated with raisins and sultanas that Ring couldn't really understand where their eyes were. He didn't recognise any of them, though. Having seen "Drop-Dead" earlier, he thought there might be a few more legends called in for the try-out day. A slight twinge of disappointment.

The group were called in, with the previous four departing off to the left following the instructions of another member of staff. None of them seemed particularly happy.

'Are they out then?' Jam asked.

'I don't know. Looks like it.' Ring fought against a voice in his head, didn't allow himself to even think the words.

Jam must've picked up on Ring's expression.

He nudged his friend, gave him a reassuring grin, an exaggerated nod. 'Look, there was always going to be failure around you today. But you're the success in the middle of it. Yeah?'

'Yeah,' Ring nodded, 'thanks, Jam.'

'You just keep running those drills in your head, stretch out a bit. Remember any of that advice your granddad would've given you. You've got this.'

Ring heard someone laugh behind him but chose not to turn around. If they wanted a reaction, he wasn't going to give it to them. Besides, he was trying to blink back the tears. Granddough would've loved it here, in amongst all the excitement and energy. The thought of him felt so all-consuming that Ring couldn't recall any of his words of wisdom.

He had to distract himself from the rising emotion. He wished Granddough could have been here, to see what he had achieved - even at this early stage. A first-time applicant getting to attend a try-out for the Sponge Dungeon?

Way to go, Ringo! He heard in his grandfather's voice.

Jam was scribbling down on his notepad again, probably around the importance of his pep talk so he could claim some reflective glory in the future. Knowing Jam, he'd probably say that was the moment that changed everything.

So what? Let him have his slice of history, Ring shrugged.

The line moved forward again, another four allowed to pass between the twin sentinels. Ring chose not to look out for how many were disappearing off to the left.

'You four are next,' one of the cupcakes said, jabbing a finger forward at a fruit scone, a sponge roll, Ring, and Jam.

'Oh, no. Sorry, I'm not... There's been a mistake. I'm just a journalist,' Jam said.

'No journalists. Out. Now,' the other cupcake said.

'Sorry, no. I'm a journalist but more here in a sort of friendship capacity today. Supporting him.' Jam put his arm around Ring, who could already feel heat rising behind his face and across his body.

'No friends. This isn't daycare. Out. Now.'

Jam looked at Ring, who half-shrugged. Ultimately, if they said Jam had to go, he had to go. Ring didn't need this now, either.

'You've got this, Ring,' Jam said, palms in the air before the cupcake could order him to leave again. 'I'll see you back at the lift. I'll wait up top. If I'm *allowed*, that is.'

Ring gave him a thumbs up, and Jam walked back, ignoring the arrowed signs as he did so.

'You-' the left cupcake pointed behind Ring, '-you're next.'

'I know,' whoever it was said, 'I can count.'

Ring turned around, sort of recognised the face. A slice of plain sponge, golden crumb and a browned exterior, thicker on her right hand side and thinner on her left, a wedge shape that Ring hadn't often encountered in Alacrumba. The white butter icing in the middle contrasted with a deep, red jam just below and gave the illusion that she had two mouths.

'Do you want me to hold your hand now your friend has gone?' She said, staring Ring dead in the eyes.

'What? No. What?' Ring stammered. Had he annoyed her just by turning around? Was she just trying to get in his head?

'You may as well go with him now.'

Ring decided not to respond and faced the cupcakes. Tried to make eye contact with them and shake his head, though he couldn't see their eyes behind their black sunglasses.

'I hope you box better than you talk,' she said.

Ring tried to think of something to say but was interrupted by the foghorn call of 'Next'. The cupcakes parted and gestured for the four of them to move forward.

Ring suddenly felt heavy and light at the same

time - as though he could sink through the table or float up above it. He could hear everything and nothing, and his eyes seemed to dry out as he stared ahead, even if they didn't really register anything.

This is it. The first step, he reminded himself, even as the cake behind him pushed past, her thick right side nudging into him. *Focus.*

There was no ring.

No ropes, no turnbuckles. No training dummies or trainers holding pads. No punchbags or weights or skipping ropes. No walls or ceiling. No arena. No fanfare. No Victor Sponge or Fred Velvet.

Just four black mats laid out next to each other, facing the table with the panel behind.

The bored voice of the chocolate cake came through a megaphone that, given the proximity, was really not needed.

'Please present your numbered cards. You are all boxers with no professional experience, so this is a preliminary test to determine if your basics are of the appropriate standard to begin your try-out at the Sponge Dungeon. You will listen to the commands and perform the combinations as requested. We will judge you on your execution. Understood?'

Ring nodded, held up his number. He was at

the end of the line, with the cake next to him (121), and the sponge roll (110) and fruit scone (132) completing the line-up.

So that's why, Ring realised as he saw all their numbers were three-digits long. They'd been funnelling the newer fighters to a specific training area. He tried to push down the thought that this was a 'preliminary test', but it nibbled at the edge of his conscience. What if he failed here? Could he even say he had attended if he never made it to the first proper challenge?

Ring latched on to a passing thought - any passing thought - to distract himself from the overwhelming fear of failure, and found that he couldn't help but wonder what Janice's record was. He had imagined she'd never even donned a pair of gloves, let alone had at least one professional bout. She also didn't mention any previous fight experience. He felt vindicated in his distrust towards her and her happy-go-lucky, giggly attitude. She would, presumably, be going through her first test now; probably running drills with Victor Sponge himself. Probably some sort of local legend in Bisconsin.

Ring found a bitterness in himself that he didn't know he had.

Focus, he reminded himself, having realised he had no idea what the chocolate cake had just said.

He copied everyone else and placed his number at the front of his mat, facing the judges, and stretched a little, jumped on the spot to loosen his body up. *This is your day. Your destiny.*

'You look nervous,' 121 smirked to his left.

He didn't dignify her with a response, instead opened his bag and pulled on his blue boxing gloves, fastening them as tight as he could around his wrists, wiggling his fingers inside.

Ring was the only one who put gloves on, the others opting for bare fists. Truthfully, he had no idea why he was putting them on. Should he take them off? No. He'd always visualised having the referee raise his hand in the air, and in those visualisations he always saw the blue gloves, the "Recipe for Success" branding on the straps, the shimmer of the gold lettering, and the gentle accent of the pink laces raised high, being snapped by a thousand flashbulb cameras; captured by a million pairs of eyes.

So what if it was just him? He had to follow his own path.

'Stances. Ready?' It was the deep, husky voice of the fruit cake - though it wasn't so much a question as it was a warning. 'Begin!'

Four fists flew forwards, synchronised to the very moment the words came out of the fruit cake's mouth. She had no need for the megaphone, instead barking orders from behind the desk with authority.

Ring listened intently, his body reacting instinctively. He jabbed before she'd even said to jab; hit a picture-perfect left cross that snapped powerfully through the air. He was tense but tense was good, tense was focused and responsive. Alert.

'Right hook.'

Ring twisted his body then put all his power into performing a delicious, textbook hook. It was hard to know where to stop without a punchbag or a pad to hit, but he felt like he showed strength and skill, good control. He caught sight of the wedge of sponge cake next to him, felt a flash of grudging admiration for how impressive her form was. Her punches snapped and her expression was still so light, so confident. Fluid, one move flowing into another with ease.

'Left hook.'

Ring did the same again, a big twist into a punch that would've even knocked the "King" down during any of their ghost-spars in his apartment.

'Jab-straight-jab-jab.'

He whistled through the moves, and he could tell he was just a bit out of time with everyone else.

Focus!

'Uppercut-uppercut.'

Which hand? It didn't matter, he threw a right and a left, moving from a low base to a good extension on the right, fluidly into the left, throwing a bit of head movement in for good measure. Not quite his signature "Glazed Over", but not far off.

He found himself back in rhythm now. Squashed his doubt about that jabbing combination. In a fight, things would go wrong, punches wouldn't work. Plans would change when he got hit in the face - so what would he do then? Panic and give up? Or keep fighting, keep throwing punches, find a way to win?

'Bob and weave.'

Ring had to stop himself throwing a punch, styling into a sort of rolling figure of eight. He had to crouch down into the weave but he was certain it looked impressive as he pushed himself to sway to the extremes. He nearly bumped heads with number 121, and he was sure he heard her curse him under her breath.

This brought a wry smile to his face.

The instructions stopped and Ring noticed he was the only one still weaving, still low. The others were now throwing a variety of punches, all at different times and speeds, but all with the same high intensity, different grunts of effort.

He cursed himself for not listening, not focusing earlier; but he began to throw his own punches now.

Right-handed jabs into a straight-cross-straight.

Two jabs into a hook, another jab, now a short, sharp uppercut.

A feint (he hoped they'd like that) before a vicious, crisp left hand snapped into the space between him and the panel. He heard Walter Waffle in his head, speaking excitedly as he showed off his skills, his raw talent; heard Granddough cooing as he fired off an array of whistling, alternating straights.

He shimmied backwards, pretending to avoid some vicious counter punches, then connected with a big, dangerous series of hooks to the body, culminating in one to the head. He was sure that had impressed the lemon muffin, who was watching him and scribbled something down.

'Stop,' fog-horned the fruit cake.

The four of them came to a crashing halt, and Ring could hear the sound of heavy breathing, feel the gentle shaking and warmth in his arms and legs. The air around them still swirled and twisted.

Please, he begged, crossing his fingers inside the gloves.

Ring fought with himself - should he look

tired? Should he look happy, confident? Desperate? Was it better to be stoic and non-plussed? He wished he knew what he looked like at that point.

From the corner of his eye, he could see 121 and she appeared just as she had the whole day so far: a level of self-assuredness that he found both enviable and irritating.

Was she even *that* good?

'Number 121, please continue to your right,' chocolate cake announced.

Evidently, she was. Ring did not look at her as she picked up her bag, but he heard her say something and imagined it wasn't well-wishes or a message of good luck or commiserations for the three that remained.

Lemon muffin pointed to their paper.

'Number 103, you too. 110, 132: better luck next time. Please exit to the left.'

It took a moment for Ring to remember to move.

'Thank you,' he said, bowing to the three of them. None were looking at him, but Ring felt better for doing it all the same. A massive smile stretched across his face. He scooped up his things awkwardly into his bag, his gloves making him a bit clumsier than he'd like to be, and scurried off in the direction that 121 had just gone.

A thick arm stopped him.

'Hey mate, well done. Go get 'em in the next round for me, will ya?' 110, the sponge roll, patted him on the back, smiled.

'You got it,' Ring replied.

He breathed out heavily and proceeded to follow the sponge cake from about five paces behind. He had no desire to catch up with her. She was stopped by another pair of heavy-set cupcakes draped in black (where did they find these guards?) and waited, fiddled with his bag until he'd noticed she'd moved on again.

'Number.'

Another demand. Why did nobody just ask nicely?

Ring held up his number card and the cupcake that had remained silent pulled out a pen. They proceeded to draw a big, red, smiley face in the middle of the '0'; then scribbled a signature on the back of the card.

'Congratulations,' the artist said, 'make sure you show that at the next desk. It means you've based the basic tests.'

'Thank you,' Ring half-laughed, looking at the doodle.

'Make sure you keep that. Might be worth something someday,' the artist grinned. They caught an elbow to the mid-section for that from their colleague.

Ring nodded, thanked them again, and walked on - now a good number of steps behind 121 - but immensely curious about what artwork, if any, she had received.

A path was marked by silver stanchions with a mismatch of string, rope, and tape between them in a variety of colours. Before he wound his way around the back of the Sponge Dungeon, Ring turned and saw the next four boxers filter in. They looked nervous. He didn't imagine any of them would be following him through to the next stage.

He smiled. Even though nobody could see him here, at the back of the great black cylinder. Even though he had only just got to the real start line. Even though he was absolutely knackered from an evening of no sleep and an intense round of testing, a do-or-die display that had seen him survive to make it to the first test proper.

A huge grin, as broad as he'd ever managed in his whole life. He pumped his fists, made a sort of squeal through the gritted teeth of his smile. Felt a fuzziness spread from the hole in his centre to his whole body.

'Nice one, Ring,' he said to himself, slapping a gloved hand on his leg with a motivational grunt. *Now the real test begins. You've got this.*

Round 4:

Main Course

Two tables, two more unenthusiastic staff members, and two presentations of his number later - one of which included a comment about the smiley face being 'classic Brian' - and Ring Doughnut was now stood next to an actual, real life boxing ring. It had only taken an entire morning, but he was where he needed to be at last.

He'd spiralled around the Sponge Dungeon so many times today that he wasn't sure which ring it was. He could see the egg lift - was it the only egg lift, though? - so he looked in that direction to try and see Jam, but with no luck. His friend had probably found someone interesting to talk to, or got bored of waiting and gone home.

Maybe he's consoling Janice, Ring thought. He still couldn't believe she'd had at least one bout before. Well, if his logic was right, anyway. There could've been all manner of queues for inexperienced fighters.

So, the positive news was that Ring Doughnut was within touching distance of a genuine, bona fide, state-of-the-art boxing ring for the first time in his life. The ropes were thicker than he thought they'd be, and actually looked more like chunky cables covered in black rubber. They didn't look as stretchy as he had expected either. The mat wasn't as pristine grey as it appeared from afar. It was a patchwork of different greys and scuffs in the centre, with only the parts beneath the ropes still a light grey that could almost pass for white. And those turnbuckle pads which had looked to be a deep red? Well, those actually were deep red.

At least he'd got something right.

The less positive news was that, despite his best efforts to get away from the sponge cake, he was still behind her. He'd hung back a bit to try and avoid any further engagement, and even though that strategy had worked so far, Ring couldn't shake the feeling that she was just waiting for her moment; stalking him, somehow, despite the fact that he was the one who was following her. He really couldn't be bothered with another cutting remark, or to struggle to find a comeback of his own again, and he really didn't want his day to be defined with how well he'd traded barbs with some random slice of cake.

She's no better than you, Ring. She was at the no-bout try-out too, he reminded himself.

The trainers had apparently stopped for a short break. There was a general chatter around the dozen or so boxers stood by this particular ring. Ring didn't join in, but he was listening; realised that those with experience had also had to take a 'preliminary test'.

'Yeah, this guy absolutely nailed me the first time - but then I got him with like, three-in-a-row, so it was pretty quick. But tough start,' he heard a deep voice behind him say.

Ring would've turned around to ask what exactly they'd had to do, but wouldn't that reveal he wasn't there, and had in fact got no experience at all? What if that then made him an easy target this round? Better to keep some mystery, some secrecy. At least until he knew what this test would be.

Not that I'm ashamed. They all had no experience at some point.

Annoyingly, 121 didn't seem to have peace and harmony on her agenda.

He heard her mock someone ahead for the huge swollen eye they already had.

'You're celebrating getting here, to *this* point?'

She scoffed. 'Wow, how ambitious. This is the easy bit. Even a bread roll could've made it here.'

It was a blueberry muffin, number 33, bearing the brunt of her criticism.

'You need to lighten up,' they said.

She continued, 'Maybe if you lightened up, you wouldn't be so easy to hit. Look like you're a few grammes too heavy to me. I'd love to meet you in the next round. I'd make your eyes match.'

The muffin laughed, turned away - but not before Ring had seen a flash of anger across their face.

She's in their head, he warned himself. That's what she was after - a reaction, a foothold. Something she could use later, just in case. All this bravado, all this stinging criticism and nasty comments - purely so she could get an advantage.

Ring wouldn't stand for it. He decided he'd play her at her own game.

'Hey,' he said, almost tapping her on the shoulder but realising he still had his gloves on, quickly hiding them behind his back. No need to provide an easy target.

'Oh, *you're* here? No way you got through. You couldn't even throw a half-decent jab,' she said, her eyes rolling.

'I can't believe it either,' Ring said, a huge grin baked onto his face.

'You should probably pack up before the next set. You won't make it.'

'Oh? I'm only here for fun, really. Just figured it would be a good thing to say I've done, y'know?' Ring hated saying it, would've hated to see someone so dismissive, so casual about such a huge event.

He was willing to bet she would see it that way, too.

She scowled at him. She was shorter than Ring by a head, but she glared into his eyes the whole time, trying to bore another hole through him.

'My name's Ring Doughnut,' he said, extending a hand. Forgetting about the gloves again.

'Why are you still wearing those? Seriously...' She looked around, tried to attract other eyes, to embarrass Ring. The others didn't seem to care, though; some were even wearing gloves of their own. 'Ring Doughnut, eh? Good job that name's easy to forget.'

'I guess so.' *Is it?*

A brief pause, but neither of them turned away.

'What did you want?' 121 asked. She still had a half-smirk on her face; a condescending look that made Ring shrink inside.

'Just to chat, pass the time. Everyone else is.

Thought it might be nice to make friends,' he lied. 'We could cheer each other on?'

'I don't need a cheer squad, and I don't think any amount of cheering is going to make you good enough. You need to go back to your coach.'

'I'm my own coach.' Ring didn't know why he said that. Wished he hadn't immediately.

She laughed at him. She laughed loud. High-pitched, a cackle.

Then she turned around. He'd been dismissed.

Ring realised others had stopped talking and were looking at him now. He wished he could just disappear under the apron for a while, let everyone go back to their conversations. He felt the heat of the sun on his face again, high in sky outside the window, and the heat inside him, and he wished he'd never said a word.

And that, Ring, is why you need to focus. On. Your. Own. Game. It wasn't even as though the blueberry muffin had turned around and recognised him. Ring hadn't helped anyone, only hindered himself. *Don't get involved in these stupid exchanges.*

Fortunately, there was movement again in the ring. A fresh batch of the security cupcakes arrived, daubed in black cases that looked like suits, with one placing a wooden stool in the corner of the ring, and another dropping a black punchbag with a thud.

The third scanned around the ring quickly, then held open the ropes for a striking red, diminutive figure to roll into the ring.

"Drop-Dead" Fred Velvet, Ring gasped, *I'm going to train with "Drop-Dead" Fred Velvet!*

Ring could barely keep up with the trainer's instructions, so he was glad to still be outside the ring. Watching. Acclimatising. The bright red cake spoke at such speed, swallowing the words and merging them into each other, a stream of gibberish punctuated by the sound of gloves hitting the black pads on his palms, the *ffooft* of air and the grunt of effort.

He watched as a custard cream was sent home.

The blueberry muffin, almost twice the size of Fred Velvet, was sent away with tears falling from their swollen eyes. Ring thought it was a bit unfair they didn't get someone taller in to do the sparring, watching the muffin have to lean down and into every strike. Even so, they weren't quick enough: missing a few snap-shots, catching a couple of counters. That session was over almost before it had started.

As a shortbread got in the ring to try, it was just number 121 ahead of Ring. Again, he tried to look elsewhere - noted that the queues were still going strong even though it must have been mid-afternoon by now. He felt tired, wished he'd got some more sleep last night. What if that cost him?

'Stop worrying,' he muttered to himself.

'You're not getting in anyway,' 121 sneered, still facing away.

'How would you know?'

She cackled again, high and wicked.

The shortbread was sent out as quickly as they'd entered, throwing just a single punch at the bag before being directed to leave. Ring had to wonder what they'd done so wrong so quickly; was annoyed he hadn't watched them in case he could've learned something.

"Drop-Dead" called for the next fighter, and 121 hopped up on to the apron and ducked under the ropes.

'Uncle Fred,' 121 said, casting a sly look back at Ring.

'Oh, hello Vicky,' the red cake grinned. 'Your dad told me to expect you.'

'It's dumb he's making me do this anyway. What a waste of time.'

'What else would you be doing on a beautiful day like today?' Fred Velvet smiled.

Other try-outs had been over in less time than this. Ring felt aggrieved, angry. Not only did 121 - Vicky? - know the trainers, she was related to

Sponge himself? He could have screamed.

She hasn't even got through yet, he reminded himself. Sure, it seemed pretty obvious she would, but Ring had to put his faith in these trainers. They would need to see *something* in her, above and beyond everyone else. To not do so would just cheapen the Sponge Dungeon's name.

'Not my time. Yours. You could've had a nice day off, Uncle Fred,' Vicky said, nudging the red cake in the shoulder playfully. His arms down by his side, his expression easy, relaxed. A hearty laugh.

'Please, I'd be here anyway. Have you got your candidate number?' Fred Velvet looked at her piece of cardboard, then shook his head. 'They made you go through basic preliminary testing?'

'Oh, don't. I got the single most belligerent cupcake at sign-up. Absolutely did not understand that I had an exemption.'

'Did you get their name?' Fred Velvet passed Vicky a pair of bright cherry-red gloves with black wrist straps. They looked pristine, shiny, like a fresh glaze reflecting the fluorescent lights above.

'Don't worry. I'll sort it Uncle Fred.'

'I swear, some of the staff-' he raised an eyebrow to the outside of the ring where his entourage of cupcakes were gathered '-are absolutely useless this year. Making days like this such a pain. We'd do better not bothering and just focusing on the roster we have.'

'Try and tell that to my dad,' Vicky laughed.

Ring's fingers dug into his palms. He ground his teeth against each other and felt a knot in both his shoulders. He tapped his right foot on the floor rapidly, the knocking noise getting louder as he did so. He kept turning around but couldn't catch anyone's eye; couldn't share his frustrations with them.

But they all must have been annoyed, surely? Waiting all day, only for these two to be chatting away like old friends. Because they were old friends. Family.

Ring would've said something but he didn't want to jeopardise his own place at the Sponge Dungeon. He hoped he'd have a chance to get things off his chest later. After this test, he could confront Vicky properly.

'It's the bloody deal with the FOOD FiGHT!,' Fred Velvet said, shaking his head, 'they just want more fighters from all the gyms. Apparently, there's something in the works but we can't have the same old faces keep going up against each other.'

'You don't fancy coming out of retirement, then?' Vicky laughed again. That witch's cackle of a laugh.

'I might do if we have too many more useless boxers today,' he replied. He hadn't even tried to whisper. That one got a scoff from someone behind. Ring wasn't sure he could open his mouth without vomiting pure, unbridled frustration.

'Well, you're going to see at least one good one.'

'Lucky me,' Fred Velvet smiled, moving into position. 'Ready?'

'Are you?' Vicky smiled.

Undoubtedly, Vicky was talented.

She hadn't even been trying in the basic preliminary test, that was for sure.

Watching her spar from an orthodox stance, landing powerful punches, Ring could've been forgiven for thinking it was actually Victor Sponge in there and not his daughter. She moved in a languid way that was at odds with her shorter, stockier build; hit fast, sharp jabs, kept Fred at distance. She had stepped up her game significantly.

There's a lot more to her, Ring noted. Even with the improvement from the earlier activities, she was still moving at half-speed, still holding back. Or at least appeared to be. Was that arrogance or incompetence? Much as he wished it was the latter, Ring was sure that it was simply her exerting the minimum amount of effort required to pass this stage.

Still, her shots landed with a wheeze on the worn black-and-red pads, and she followed "Drop-Dead" Fred Velvet around the ring, closing the space. Ring could have believed this was an actual match if Fred Velvet ever threw a punch back at her. He wondered what the others who had been sent home would make of this sham of a test.

Apparently, nobody else had noticed how 'Uncle Fred' had slowed down his commands, or how passive he was, as those behind Ring kept commenting on how good Vicky Sponge looked, how slick she was, how crisp her punches landed. Was Ring the only one seeing this mockery for what it truly was?

Fred Velvet wasn't as harsh or unreadable, and even seemed to drop in words of encouragement. If he was trying to keep some unbiased exterior, it plainly wasn't working. Was she really any better than those who had gone before her? Again, Ring reminded himself that he wasn't bitter or biased, but he was merely observing, noting that any of the previous trialists would have all looked that good if they'd got the same treatment.

She launched into a flurry of punches, ending with Fred Velvet up against the ropes. He called a stop to the proceedings.

'Congratulations, Vicky. You're through to the next stage. Take this to the front of the gym and they'll take care of the rest.' He handed her a small black token with a red 'V' in the middle. 'Assume you know your way to the entrance by now.'

'You'd hope so,' she smiled, 'Thanks, Uncle Fred. See you soon.'

'I'm popping by tonight, actually, so I might catch you then. Remind your dad about it. He forgot last time.'

'He's getting too old,' Vicky laughed.

'Aren't we all?' Fred laughed, before calling out 'Next.'

As Ring entered under the ropes, he caught a glance from Vicky. That sneer was now an arrogant smile. He tried to swallow his frustration. Sure, Vicky had an unfair advantage, but he wouldn't get anywhere by letting himself be fuelled by rage and injustice. He had to be calm, cool, collected. Repeated his one-word mantra of focus, just as he had all day.

Destiny's calling. Focus.

He was surprised by how bouncy the ring was under his feet. He'd imagined it would be much sturdier, but there was a bit of give in each step, the ropes bobbling as he moved forward to meet Fred Velvet in the middle of the ring.

Vicky was still stood at ringside, watching

him. He could see her out of the corner of his eye.

Focus. Focus on you, he repeated.

'Hi, Fred, I'm-'

'-It's 'Trainer'. What's your candidate number?' *Trainer* fired back.

'Sorry. Here,' he offered his piece of cardboard; couldn't help but hear a snigger from Vicky. Why had she taken such a disliking to him? Or was this just revenge because he'd tried to get at her earlier?

I won't tell you again, Ring Doughnut. You. Need. To. Focus. On. You.

He shut his eyes, took a deep breath.

'I see you brought your own gloves,' Fred Velvet remarked. 'Quite expensive for someone who's never had a bout before.'

Ring didn't know what to say, but felt he had to say something. He searched the hard expression of Fred Velvet but didn't find a crumb of comfort. Fred was small, cube-shaped, with two thick layers of bright red sponge and a thin layer of white buttercream icing in the middle, and an even thinner layer on top. His white moustache twitched when he spoke but concealed most of his mouth, but Ring had just assumed he was snarling. He looked so similar and yet so different from the poster on Ring's wall. Not quite so even. His eyes a little harder, a little colder.

'I'm committed to boxing,' he stammered.

'Commitment would be having a match before you try-out for the most prestigious gym in the Doughjo.' Fred paused, met Ring's stare with intense eyes. 'That's how we used to do it. But what do I know?'

'I'd be happy to wear a pair of the house gloves if you'd prefer?' Ring offered.

'You see the queue? We aren't wasting time with you changing your outfit.'

'Understood. Sorry.' Ring could feel his eyes welling up, but he didn't want to cry. He wasn't upset. Not at the gloves comment, anyway. Why did his emotions feel so close to the surface?

'It's a long day, these try-outs. Hard day,' Fred Velvet said, pulling the pads back on. He chewed at his top lip. 'For everyone. Easy to get a bit short when folks are trying to punch you all day. Understand?'

Ring nodded, blinked the emotion away from the surface. He did understand. He took a deep breath, felt some tension ease from his shoulders and his back.

'Ready?'

'Yes, trainer.' Ring wondered if he'd ever sparred with "Drop-Dead" Fred Velvet before in his head, within his room on the top shelf in Alacrumba. He could imagine Waffle calling the close fight; hear Granddough talking up the history of the trainer but also the sheer skill of Ring.

He snapped back to the real world as he moved his head to avoid a quick shot with the pad from "Drop-Dead".

A stream of words came out of Fred Velvet's mouth and Ring hoped he'd understood them correctly - alternating jabs then an uppercut. He dodged two more pads thrown at him, followed with a double straight and a hook of his own. He blocked the next set, covering the side of his head, arms tight in over his body. He went for a left cross but something told him that wasn't what he was asked for - yet he knew he'd delivered it well, felt it shake through his body as he hit the pads. The feeling was exhilarating, exhausting. He felt panicked and alert. A series of jabs next, over and over and over and over and over. He then nailed a quick combination of big, powerful shots - presumably designed by Fred Velvet to mimic going in for the finish at the end of a fight - and he backed the trainer up to the ropes. Big overhands, heavy shots, fired with his full weight behind them.

Now "Drop-Dead" was advancing on him. The veteran trainer slipped around Ring, stepped on his foot, not once but twice, and he chucked a couple of shots in with the pad that Ring was able to dodge and then block with a solid guard. Ring instinctively fired a counter-punch back and the trainer was just about able to get out of the way.

Is he smiling or not?

There was no time to work that particular quandary out. More instructions came from Fred Velvet, each to be delivered at pace and with power, with precision. Ring began to notice his punches not quite hitting their mark, the sound of the pads not quite as satisfying. The trainer was on the move, wasn't simply standing still to be hit, but Ring couldn't manage a clean shot.

He heard Vicky say something from ringside, though he was too zoned in to make out the words. The noise was enough to distract him, though, and he managed to move his body so Fred Velvet's punch went through the hole in his centre.

The two of them awkwardly untangled and reset. Fred Velvet ordered him to wait behind a guard, then unleashed a torrent of jabs and straights and hooks and crosses; demanded then that Ring retaliate - and he did, throwing punches until his arms were cramping and his back hurt and his legs felt like they had no more oomph in them.

The veteran advanced again now and caught Ring's feet once more, but this time it caused Ring to stumble and get caught with a glancing blow to the side of the body. He regained his footing, threw a punch back - but got caught by another shot to the opposite side.

Now Fred Velvet was rocking and rolling, moving faster and faster from side-to-side, calling for Ring Doughnut to throw a punch, to hit him if he could.

Focus. One good punch to change your life, he reminded himself.

He waited, watched behind his own guard.

A feint with a left jab.

Straight in with a right cross.

Fred Velvet skipped back.

But not before Ring dashed his moustache, smooshing it half across the old fighter's cheek.

Fred Velvet threw up his arms to signal the end of the session.

Ring was breathing heavily, but he stood up straight and gritted his teeth.

'You did good, blue gloves,' "Drop-Dead" Fred Velvet said, removing his pads. 'But you got hit twice and I could've got you a few more times. You're not ready yet.'

Ring didn't know whether to say anything, didn't know if he could say anything as he heaved down air, but he met Fred Velvet's stare and puffed out his chest, stood tall and proud. Anything he could to look like the champion he was destined to become. To hang on to the dream. Did he have anything he could say? Literally anything at all?

'But then again, you did catch me at the end there.' Fred Velvet rubbed his face, nodded, pursed his lips tight under the smudged moustache. 'Not many land a shot - even a glancing one.'

Please. Please. Please.

It was only a moment but it lingered for an age. The space between them heavy and thick. Ring kept eye contact even though he wanted to scrunch them tight and beg for the opportunity to continue. He had done enough, though, surely? He'd landed a punch. That would be enough, right?

'Ok, blue gloves - I've decided.' *Please.* 'It's a no today. Get some fights in, have a few local bouts, a few scraps; come back in a year or two. You've got potential. Just too raw for what we're looking for at the moment. But there's a career in this for you, if you want it enough. Understand?'

'No.' Ring didn't know what he'd said. No to the year or two? No to the rejection? No, he didn't understand? No to all of it or none of it?

'This isn't one of those times where you fight back, ok? I don't change my mind. Do you know how many rejected candidates get invited back? Know how many I personally invite back? Here-' Fred Velvet offered him a white token with a black 'V' on it. '-include this with your application in two years, it'll make things a lot simpler. Now, please leave the ring.'

Ring bit the inside of his mouth. Turned to leave. Saw Vicky. Remembered what an easy session she'd had. Heat rising. He couldn't hear his own thoughts for the sound of anger bubbling up in him. She smirked. She'd had it so easy, and yet Ring was going home? He felt his throat close up, his mouth became claggy. No tears but white-hot dry eyes staring at the mat.

'No, it's not fair.' *What am I doing?* 'It's not fair that she got an easy ride and I do all that and don't get through.'

'Don't do this. Don't. I'm trying to be nice to you, blue gloves. I don't want to rescind the offer,' Fred Velvet said.

The trio of cupcakes at ringside fanned out in formation, moving to three sides of the ring, with Fred Velvet occupying the other.

'Give me another chance, please. I'm sorry, I don't want to waste your time or to disagree with you - but this is my dream. My dream. I can do this. I'll do another session. I'll do another ten sessions. I'll wait until the end of the day. Just give me another chance.' Ring felt the eyes of the others on him, started to hear murmurs and mumblings. The laughter to his left of Vicky Sponge. Fred Velvet growled opposite him.

'You get another chance next year, if you get

out the ring now. If you don't get out the ring now, this token goes back in my pocket and I'll make sure you're blacklisted. Your choice. Be smart. Passion's good but you're nothing in this game without discipline.' Fred's tone was calm but authoritative; understanding but commanding.

Another time, Ring might've listened.

Another time, where the world was fairer. Where Vicky Sponge hadn't been such an insufferable opponent, full of her own arrogance. Maybe, if she wasn't so nasty, he would have left the ring and wished her the best.

Another time, where rumours of Cassius Cake's potential retirement weren't so prevalent. Even if he didn't believe them, the "King" couldn't go on forever. What if Ring was wrong about the next match being his last?

Another time, when he could have gone back home and talked it through with Granddough, worked on his weaknesses with his grandfather's expertise there to guide him.

But he couldn't.

This wasn't another time.

This was his time.

'You gave her-' he pointed a gloved hand at Vicky, still sneering, '-an easy test. She isn't any better than me. You can't honestly say she did better in the boxing session than I did.' He believed his words and spoke them with fire and conviction.

'Oh did I?' Fred Velvet said, stepping up to him, chest to chest. The token was nowhere to be seen now.

'I deserve a fair chance. Everyone here does. So I want to be retested - or I want her to be given the proper test. If I'm not worthy of the Sponge Dungeon, then she definitely isn't - even if she is Victor Sponge's daughter.' Ring's voice cracked a bit but he maintained eye contact.

His eyes were locked with Fred Velvet's for an age. Neither trainer nor candidate said anything. Clenched jaws. Ring could hear a beating in his head that seemed to emanate from behind his eyes, but he stood firm. He wasn't sure he even blinked. Deadlock.

The steely exchange was broken by movement in his periphery. Ring looked away but he still felt Velvet's fiery stare locking him in place.

'Let's play a game then,' Vicky said, rolling under the bottom of the five black ropes around the ring. 'You and me, three rounds. Winner gets this.' She held up the black token with the red 'V' between two fingers.

'No need for that, Vicky. Security can handle it,' said Fred Velvet, still encroaching on Ring's personal space. 'He's not got the discipline to become a student of the dungeon.'

'It's fine, Uncle Fred. He's disrespected you. He's disrespected my family. And worst of all,' she moved closer to him now, that grin still stuck to her face, 'he's disrespected me. I intend to teach him a very harsh lesson.'

"Drop-Dead" Fred Velvet waved off the security cupcakes - who were now on the apron and looking increasingly likely to drag Ring out - but the veteran fighter stayed tight to Ring's body; kept his beady eyes fixed on Ring, his breath still hot on Ring's chest.

'You're on,' Ring said, only now stepping back from the trainer.

'Great, Uncle Fred will score the contest.'

'That's not fair,' Ring protested.

'Trust me, when we're done: you'll know you lost.'

Ring wished Granddough had been there. Even Jam or Janice. Anyone to just be in his corner. He briefly wished he'd just left quietly, like the others had before him. Why hadn't he?

Because it's your destiny.

He wondered if Fred Velvet was going to hold a grudge against him, if - no, *when* - he beat Vicky and joined the Sponge Dungeon. Ring could well imagine the old trainer being the sort to never forget that he'd had his judgement questioned. To grill him for the rest of time, to always undermine him. Never put him forward for big events or title shots.

He wondered if Vicky Sponge would actually hand over the token; if Fred Velvet would let her. He had to trust they'd hold out their end of the deal, especially with ringside witnesses.

Just like we trained for, he smiled. *Pretend it's just another one of your shadow-boxing sessions. Make yourself undeniable.*

'Right then. Let's do this,' Vicky said, re-fastening her gloves with the help of her uncle. 'Try and make it past the first round.'

Proving Grounds

Unofficial bout

WAFFLE: Welcome one and all on a glorious day here in Calorifornia for a glimpse into the future. Two fighters with plenty of potential are going to battle it out for the single spot available in the next round of the try-outs here at this, one of the most hallowed halls of boxing, the Sponge Dungeon.

Joining me at the desk today, as always, is Ring Doughnut's coach and trainer, and one of the Doughjo's greatest 'what if?' stories: it's Granddough.

GRANDDOUGH: Thank you for your kind introduction, Wally.

WAFFLE: And, of course, it's the dough ball who could've won it all: Bazz.

BAZZ: A pleasure to watch Ring Doughnut lose here.

GRANDDOUGH: Ha! Cheeky little… We're going to have fun today, aren't we, Bazz?

WAFFLE: Anyway, a big match today with a lot on the line for both contenders. How do you see it going, chaps?

GRANDDOUGH: Big match for Ringo. Sorry, Ring Doughnut. He's got to prove the doubters wrong - and one of those doubters is Fred Velvet, so it's a big ask. But he can do it. He's powerful, accurate; could be quicker, sure, but he's got good fundamentals.

WAFFLE: And how do you rate the other rookie's chances? Vicky Sponge was sent through on merit.

BAZZ: I'll provide the unbiased commentary then, shall I? Vicky Sponge isn't here on merit. She knows the trainer. She'll still be too good for that con-artist Doughnut, though.

GRANDDOUGH: I don't agree with Bazz but he makes a good point. Vicky Sponge does know the trainer, so, if I'm Ringo, I know I've got to knock her out within three rounds or her old uncle is gonna send her through. It's what I'd do for him, if I'm honest. He's in enemy territory here and he knows it.

WAFFLE: What can Doughnut do to mitigate that feeling of having everyone against him?

GRANDDOUGH: Well, normally you'd have a crowd up against you, too. Fortunately, I think most of those here aren't really pulling for either fighter, so he doesn't need to win them over or shut them up.

That being said, he has to make his mark on the fight early. The first round: get something on her, see if you can get a wobble, see if you can make her a bit less sure of herself. He can do it, but he has to believe and he has to make sure he takes any chance he gets.

WAFFLE: This will be Ring Doughnut's first time boxing against an actual opponent. First time between the ropes, going toe-to-toe with someone else who wants to knock him out. How will he cope on his debut, Bazz?

BAZZ: Wally, debuts are tough. You wanna put on a show, wanna make a statement - and most of these kids do, y'know? They get a handpicked opponent, a local jobber, and they knock 'em down a couple of times and the ref calls the fight off.

Here, we've got two rookies who want to make it. Sure, this won't count to their professional record - but it might well mean the difference between ever becoming a professional or not. I've seen folks lose that spark after losing their first match. This could be brutal. Life-defining.

WAFFLE: Life-defining indeed. Now, normally, we'd have some more fighter statistics, a tale of the tape, for you ahead of this fight but the impromptu nature of it means we're left to our own observations.

Ring Doughnut the taller of the two but Vicky Sponge is the denser, and she is of   course backed by a huge family legacy. Boxing is in every crumb of her being. Vicky Sponge operates with an orthodox stance, leading with her left hand, whilst Ring Doughnut is a southpaw. Does that give him an advantage?

GRANDDOUGH: Y'know, given neither of them have experience, I don't think it does. Normally, you fight a lot of orthodox boxers - but if you've never had a match before, then coming up against something a bit different isn't actually different at all. So no, I don't think there's any benefit in this specific moment.

WAFFLE: Fred Velvet now checking the gloves on both competitors and we're almost ready. Any pre-fight predictions as to how this'll go?

GRANDDOUGH: I don't do predictions, Wally. All I'll say is he - he being Ring Doughnut, of course - needs to knock her down or knock her out. He'll know that, and he needs to back himself. Believe in himself. You got this, Ringo!

BAZZ: They're both frauds. Hope Sponge knocks him out fast.

Ding!

WAFFLE: Here we go then in round one of this three-round contest. Ring Doughnut starting out from the left-hand side in the blue shorts and blue gloves, and with the southpaw stance; while Vicky Sponge is wearing red gloves and black shorts, coming in from the right-hand side as we look at it, orthodox stance.

GRANDDOUGH: Classic boxing, blue versus red.

WAFFLE: It's Sponge occupying the centre of the ring here, with Doughnut moving around the outside. Tentative start with neither fighter throwing a punch yet. A couple of feints but you sense that when they start, they won't stop.

GRANDDOUGH: Watch out for that leading right hand from Doughnut. He's got a quick jab and a strong follow-up.

BAZZ: Hits like a pillow though. No power.

WAFFLE: It is Doughnut who throws that jab first but he just meets Sponge's guard, throws another without a lot of force behind it. He won't get points for those, but it looks like he's trying to find his range. He's got the reach advantage in this one.

BAZZ: Reach advantage is so important. If I'd been taller, I'd have won so many more times in my career. It's tough having to close all the time, although Sponge seems content to stay rooted in the middle.

WAFFLE: Doughnut now with another jab and he follows this one up with a textbook right-straight that finds the guard again but a solid combination from the youngster. He goes for the jab ag- Oh!

BAZZ: Yes!

WAFFLE: Vicky Sponge throws a haymaker that has Ring Doughnut stepping backwards to the ropes. Wow! What power in that.

GRANDDOUGH: That'll put doubt in Ringo's head. First punch she's thrown and it connected beautifully. Ring looked to be getting settled, but she's responded with a huge shot out of nowhere. No wind-up on it, either, so rest assured she can hit that harder.

WAFFLE: Sponge doesn't press the advantage but you can see she's smiling behind her gloves.

GRANDDOUGH: That'll get to him, no doubt.

WAFFLE: Doughnut is coming back at her now though, throws another jab but he's ducking back almost before he's fully extended. Sponge seems to have really spooked him with just a single punch.

GRANDDOUGH: It's tough, he's got to re-find his belief here. He got hit. For the first time ever: he got hit. Now hit back.

WAFFLE: More tentative work from Ring Doughnut, the busier of the two fighters so far - but he's seeing little success in breaking through the Sponge guard. He goes low this time but Sponge steps back, retaliates with a heavy straight and a jab, and Doughnut does well to cover up.

Sponge now pressing forward. She catches him with a hook to the body and gets a punch in on the face and another on the shoulder. Ring Doughnut can't seem to keep up.

GRANDDOUGH: She isn't throwing that many punches, and they aren't coming quickly, but they are deliberate. Accurate. Doughnut's got to work out the pattern, the order of the combinations or he may as well head out of the ring right now.

BAZZ: They're hurting him. He's so awkward out there, hasn't got a clue how to respond. You might want to start worrying now, old-timer.

GRANDDOUGH: Ha!

WAFFLE: Counter-punch by Ring Doughnut is swatted away and Vicky Sponge has closed in and nails him with some gut-punches from close range. Doughnut's gasping for air, he catches Sponge with a couple of shots to her thicker, right-hand side. She backs off but the damage must've already been done there to Doughnut.

BAZZ: Surprised she didn't open a second hole up there. That was a nasty series of blows there. Nasty.

WAFFLE: Ring Doughnut is hugging the ropes and he's just trying to stay away from Vicky Sponge right now. She's closing in again and misses with a straight but Doughnut can't capitalise. A jab back from Doughnut but there's not a lot behind it.

Ding!

WAFFLE: Well, that's the first round for both of these fighters. How did they fare, Granddough?

GRANDDOUGH: Look, Sponge won that round comfortably, no doubt about it. That's the bad news if you're a Ring Doughnut fan.

BAZZ: Is there such a thing?

GRANDDOUGH: The good news is that's the first round done. He caught her, he was finding his range. He took some heavy shots but he's still standing, he's still in this. Endurance and perseverance are just as important as power and accuracy. Two rounds to go, he needs to win both - which will be tough in enemy territory - or knock her out, like I said at the start. The equation hasn't changed for the kid.

WAFFLE: Can he do it?

GRANDDOUGH: Of course! Ring Doughnut said he's going to the very top and he's determined to get there. Even the greats like myself and Cassius Cake have lost rounds. It's about the response. The absolute best boxers find a way to respond to these setbacks. Not always in the next round, but over the course of the bout. That's what's gonna be tricky for Ringo here - he can't wait another round trying to find his range or picking Sponge off with decent jabs. He needs to find something immediately, in just his second ever round of an actual match. Ringo has to believe that's possible though, Wally. If he doesn't believe he can still win, he may as well head home now.

WAFFLE: No coaches or trainers for either fighter today, just a brief standing rest in the corner to think about the round that has just been; the round that is still to come.

Vicky Sponge has stared at Ring Doughnut the entire time, a big smile across her face. She looks comfortable and confident. For his part, Ring Doughnut has had his eyes closed and seems to be muttering something to himself.

GRANDDOUGH: Visualising his success in the next round. Focusing.

BAZZ: Wishing he was anywhere but here. You gonna ask me for any insight, Wally? Or is this desk not interested in facts?

WAFFLE: Is there anything you wanted to add?

BAZZ: Ring Doughnut sucks. He's going down in this round.

GRANDDOUGH: Excellent analysis, Bazz. If only you were this sharp as a boxer.

WAFFLE: Let's move on, shall we?

I say it all the time, but all either fighter needs is one good punch. That's it. One good punch to change his life, to advance to the next round of the try-outs today. To keep his dream alive.

Ding! Ding!

WAFFLE: Here we go then, round two of three and, if our scorecards to be believed, it's a round that Ring Doughnut in the blue gloves needs to win.

He's started off brightly, making his move to the centre of the ring to deny Vicky Sponge, and he's already throwing punches. Solid one-two combinations, though again it has to be said that they don't look to be really troubling his opponent who is content to block them off.

GRANDDOUGH: Alright, Wally, jeez. Cut him some slack, he's trying something. You sound like Bazz.

WAFFLE: No offence intended, and this may work nicely as Vicky Sponge is backed into the ropes and is having to react a bit more now. She had dictated the tempo in the first round but Doughnut is forcing her to fire back, and she's missing the mark.

GRANDDOUGH: See? This could work. Smart from Doughnut. He might be a rookie, but h-

WAFFLE: Sponge connects with a vicious hook to the side and Doughnut is staggered, and another one to the same spot. Sorry to interrupt you there, Granddough, but what a shot. A big grimace on Doughnut's face and he's trying to put the distance between them again, but it does mean that he cedes the centre of the ring back to Sponge.

BAZZ: Can't even stick with a basic strategy against another amateur. You couldn't make it up. How he got this opportunity is beyond me.

WAFFLE: Sponge seems happy to simply be back in the centre, but maybe misses an opportunity to really cause Doughnut some more problems.

BAZZ: She's given him time. She shouldn't have done that. You can imagine what "Drop-Dead" Fred Velvet and her dad would've done in that scenario.

WAFFLE: Ring Doughnut is back on the offensive and he looks for those steady one-two combinations again, catches Sponge on the shoulder, on the gloves. He's busier again, but needs more conviction, a bit more snap.

He wants the centre of the ring back, but Sponge doesn't back away and she is firing counters of her own. Nobody's really making much progress here, although as I say that Vicky Sponge is caught on that right-hand side again and has a little wobble.

Ring Doughnut goes for another shot to the right but he's caught, and Vicky Sponge is now closing the gap on him and this time does press the advantage. She's working the body with a variety of shots and Doughnut is trying to cover up, trying to weave his way out of it, but he's backed into the ropes and he is taking a pummelling.

Doughnut finally locks in the clinch and Fred Velvet calls for the break, sends Vicky back to her corner, but look how hard Ring Doughnut is breathing now, Granddough.

GRANDDOUGH: Not good for Ringo. Not good at all. But Vicky Sponge isn't exactly fresh. Her guard is a bit lower; her arms might be starting to feel heavier. You have to hope Ringo's noticed.

WAFFLE: Even if he has, can he take advantage of it?

GRANDDOUGH: He has to try, Wally.

BAZZ: If he loses this round, this could be his career over before it's even started, damn it!

WAFFLE: Forward he comes again and he's using that reach once more, but this time he's moving quickly around the outside of the ring, starting to force Sponge to circle. He catches Vicky Sponge with a solid jab, another one, and now a cross. Gets away before she can respond.

GRANDDOUGH: See? She's slowing down.

WAFFLE: Indeed, Vicky Sponge - probably a

slight favourite before the fight due to her family's history - doesn't seem to have as much fire in those fists as she did before. She's breathing heavily and looks tired. She tries a combination of her own, but Doughnut does enough to avoid them and land a response. Enough to keep her thinking.

GRANDDOUGH: Doughnut's got her now. You can't be flagging in the second round. He just needed to figure out hi-

WAFFLE: -Ring Doughnut is staggered! He landed a jab but Vicky Sponge roared forward, a huge straight that went all the way through and catches him flush in the face, then another follow up around the head and he's on jelly legs here.

BAZZ: Is this the end?

WAFFLE: Vicky Sponge with two jabs to the face, and Ring Doughnut needs to lift his guard or it'll all be over. Doughnut tries to land one back but he's caught a third massive shot, this one on the chin.

BAZZ: It's done. He's finished!

GRANDDOUGH: Stay on your feet, Ringo!

WAFFLE: Four, five now! Oh, this is a torrent from Vicky Sponge, a late flurry not dissimilar to the "Birthday Bumps" used by Cassius Cake. Ring Doughnut is still offering some sort of resistance, still hitting back at her. Not a lot on the shots but they are connecting, they will count. Huge heart, huge desire.

GRANDDOUGH: He must just be thinking that he doesn't-

Ding! Ding!

GRANDDOUGH: I was saying, he must be thinking that he doesn't want to lose here, Wally. He's stayed up on willpower alone.

BAZZ: He's stayed up because she can't generate any power. Useless.

WAFFLE: The bell there drawing an end to the second round, both fighters still standing despite trading some big shots in the previous three minutes. Both were rocked, both did some rocking. How did you score it, Granddough?

GRANDDOUGH: That one's close. I might be tempted to give it to the busier fighter but Sponge closed the round out in style, and it might only be the bell that saved Ringo. It could be two rounds to nothing in favour of the home town fighter.

WAFFLE: So Doughnut needs a knock-out here?

BAZZ: Hello? I'm still here. He needs a knock-out but he won't get it, and he's two rounds down. Don't listen to the old fool.

GRANDDOUGH: Going back to what you asked, Wally: he's got it in him, we've seen in the training sessions that he can hit hard, but he needs to do it now. Needs to do it in the ring.

WAFFLE: What would your strategy be then, Granddough?

GRANDDOUGH: Hit her hard and hit her lots.

WAFFLE: As easy as that? Ha.

BAZZ: Far be it for me to agree with my not-so-esteemed colleague - but that's the game sometimes, Wally. Sure, you can tippy-tappy your combinations, you can go to win on points, make sure you land meaningful shots and don't get hit. I like that strategy. But last round, when you're level or even behind on points and the judges don't have any reason to give you the benefit of the doubt? Swing. Swing like there's no tomorrow - 'cause there might not be, y'know?

WAFFLE: They both look tired in their corners. Ring Doughnut has a swollen lip, blackened eye; but Vicky Sponge looks the more fatigued of the two, she's still breathing heavy, the smirk isn't there this time.

A penny for the thoughts of Fred Velvet, whose expression is giving nothing away. Is there any chance that "Drop-Dead" gives Ring Doughnut a token just for his effort here?

BAZZ: Fred Velvet? No chance. No chance. No way. I'm telling you, he's fair but he's stubborn. He doesn't want to change his mind. Besides, what's the point in giving Ring a token if he loses? There's only one spot up for grabs at the end of the day. It'd just be delaying the inevitable.

GRANDDOUGH: Ringo cannot rely on anyone here but himself. Start throwing your shots. See what happens.

Ding! Ding! Ding!

WAFFLE: The final round of three in this unofficial try-out match, held just outside the Sponge Dungeon in glorious early afternoon sun.

Ring Doughnut has it all to do to beat Vicky Sponge, but the fighter in the blue gloves is starting out hot and he has closed right in on his opponent again, putting the pressure on with some measured right-hands.

GRANDDOUGH: Great start, he's tied Sponge up in her guard already. Nice work.

WAFFLE: He's mixing up those combos as well, going for a few big shots in a row. Less work behind the jab but can he keep the pace up?

BAZZ: Throwing heavy hook after hook is going to tire him out soon enough.

GRANDDOUGH: Might break Sponge first.

WAFFLE: Vicky Sponge is indeed leaning on the ropes, trying her best to move around the ring and away from the onslaught but Ring Doughnut will not be denied here. As I say that, Doughnut catches one in return and he's backed off a bit.

GRANDDOUGH: No!

WAFFLE: Doughnut comes back in but catches another to that swollen right eye. He has to shake it off, keep advancing, keep trying to find that one good punch.

BAZZ: He's let her off the hook there.

WAFFLE: Sponge manages to get a clinch in place, and Fred Velvet asks them to separate and return to their corners.

GRANDDOUGH: He'll be straight back to it though. Temporary respite for Sponge.

WAFFLE: He takes a jaw-shaker though, and another. Vicky Sponge winds up and that haymaker has him teetering. Jab, quick jab and- Oh! He's down!

GRANDDOUGH: That's a push. Vicky Sponge pushed him.

WAFFLE: He's back to his feet quickly and there's no count, so no indication that Fred Velvet is saying that was a knock-down but that is a scare for Ring Doughnut and only he will know whether it was a good shot or a push.

GRANDDOUGH: I can tell you now, Wally: it was a push. Nothing legitimate about that at all.

BAZZ: Even I can't claim that's a knock-down. Shameless from Vicky Sponge.

WAFFLE: Does it make his job harder though? Is

it still possible for Doughnut to win?

GRANDDOUGH: He won't be thinking like that. Can't be. Keep swinging, that's the stuff!

WAFFLE: Now Doughnut is back on the offensive and he's trying to get through to Sponge. Vicky Sponge looks like she's shut down, going for a win with half a round still to go but it could all change and, here we go, Ring Doughnut is turning up the pace with some quick-fire, accurate shots to the body.

GRANDDOUGH: There's a great big glove mark in the buttercream, Wally!

WAFFLE: Sponge struggling to keep pace with Doughnut as he ups the ante again, and he launches another round of savage shots. He's taking some return fire but he doesn't mind, he's grimacing his way through it.

GRANDDOUGH: He's caught her, she's down!

BAZZ: She ain't down, she's on the ropes. Get your eyes tested, ya dope.

WAFFLE: A massive uppercut, huge. Another! Some heavy-duty body shots now and Ring Doughnut has gone into overdrive. He is landing everything, Vicky Sponge isn't replying at all, she's tangled up; only on her feet because of the ropes but Fred Velvet doesn't seem to be making any effort to count here, even though she's tottering about.

BAZZ: She can't stand still! She can't see straight!

GRANDDOUGH: End it, Ring!

WAFFLE: This is bizarre. Ring Doughnut looks to Fred Velvet, but the veteran isn't indicating anything here.

GRANDDOUGH: Throw a punch, any punch. This is it!

WAFFLE: Doughnut looks confused as a dazed Vicky Sponge - barely upright, essentially sitting on the ropes at this moment - isn't being counted, but he's not throwing a punch. He seems to be indicating that she's out on her feet but she still has something of a guard. I'm not sure what he's doing here, Granddough.

BAZZ: He's throwing it away is what he's doing. Hit her!

WAFFLE: Vicky Sponge is still swaying but she's showing willing, chucking a couple of punches towards Doughnut and I wonder if that was the moment for the youngster. He's back on it now but Sponge gets out of the way nicely and clinches.

Doughnut combing back in but he catches a jab and then it is into a clinch again.

GRANDDOUGH: Oh, for the love of…

BAZZ: First smart thing Sponge has done all match.

WAFFLE: Doughnut in a tricky spot here, needing to get close enough to deliver a telling blow but stay far enough away that Sponge can't tie him up and waste valuable seconds. Only a few remain now.

This has to be it. One good punch.
GRANDDOUGH: Change your life, Ringo.
WAFFLE: One. Good. Punch.
GRANDDOUGH: He's set himself.
WAFFLE: Ring Doughnut throws himself into another uppercut… Catches her on the chin!

But Vicky Sponge has fallen into him, she's still there. She chucks one in to the mid-section; another half-hearted punch follows. She clinches.
BAZZ: Hug of death.
WAFFLE: Is there one more-

Ding! Ding! Ding!

WAFFLE: No, that's it. That's the end, the final bell rings out across the ring. Vicky Sponge immediately raises her arms in the air even as she's leaning into Ring Doughnut.

Staff are in the ring to help her back to the corner but she has got a big smile on her face, propped up against the turnbuckle. That late flurry of punches from Doughnut seemed to have her, and I'm not convinced she would've been allowed to continue in a professional fight.
GRANDDOUGH: I'm not convinced she knows

where she is right now, Wally.

WAFFLE: Doughnut not sure what to do, he's just staring at Fred Velvet. A smattering of applause from those gathered at ringside. They've seen a good, solid fight between these two. They'll be worried, knowing they've got to follow that to impress Fred Velvet and the team.

BAZZ: Should've gone the Sponge route there, Ring. Half the game is acting like you've won when you haven't. Throw your arms in the air, big grin. That sort of thing.

WAFFLE: Did he not do enough for you today then, Bazz?

BAZZ: No, obviously not. Sponge didn't either. I'm just saying he needs to act like he knows he's won. It makes the judges think about what they saw, and at the moment Vicky raising her arms and smiling, makes it look like that near KO in the last round didn't really happen.

WAFFLE: Granddough?

GRANDDOUGH: Look, the first round was definitely Vicky Sponge, no doubt. Second round: I'm going to say it's probably Vicky again, but it's close and Doughnut was the busier fighter. Third is definitely Doughnut, and should have been at least a count in there at the end - but he went down as well. So it'll depend on how Fred Velvet sees those two key moments.

BAZZ: How do we get you to admit he lost, Granddough?

GRANDDOUGH: You'd know all about losing.

WAFFLE: Well, it looks like the judge, Fred Velvet, is getting into the ring to announce a winner.

A reminder, folks, that this is not a professionally sanctioned bout and will not count to their records going forward.

BAZZ: The loser will carry this, though, Wally. There's no way they don't always have this match in the back of their head the next time they enter a ring, or pull on a pair of gloves.

WAFFLE: Fred Velvet taking his time here, he's speaking to them both at length. He is holding the prized token in his hand but has yet to give it to either competitor.

GRANDDOUGH: I can't watch.

WAFFLE: Sponge no longer smiling here.

BAZZ: Do the right thing, Fred.

WAFFLE: Ring Doughnut looks away, and-

GRANDDOUGH: -oh no-

WAFFLE: -it's Vicky Sponge who gets given the token, gets her hand raised at the end of this one.

GRANDDOUGH: Oh no.

BAZZ: Ha!

WAFFLE: A win for Vicky Sponge over Ring Doughnut after a hard-fought contest.

BAZZ: It's over for him now, Wally. Over. He's wasted his time. He can't lose his first match, he can't. What's he going to do now? Where does he go from here?

WAFFLE: A reminder it isn't an official loss.

BAZZ: No such thing as an official loss. A fight's a fight and he got beat. He will always know he lost his first match. Awful for the fraud, just awful. Look, he's already out of the ring and that might be the first and last time he ever steps between the ropes. A real sickener. I love it.

WAFFLE: Bazz, a little less hyperbole, please.

BAZZ: It's fine for you nerds with your history books saying it's just one loss, but when you've been a fighter, when you've been in the ring and felt the sting of defeat... Well, it hurts - and he hasn't got any of the sweet taste of victory to soothe him, to help minimise the pain he's feeling now, to bring him back between the ropes for another day of being punched repeatedly. This might well be it for him, Wally. I don't want him to give it up - I love seeing him get beaten around the ring - but we have to be realistic here.

WAFFLE: A sobering note, that's for sure. I think we all agree that Ring Doughnut has the potential, has the skills to go further than this. I certainly hope to see him back in the ring soon.

Unfortunately, we are out of time here. That's

all from Granddough, Bazz, and me for today after a rip-roaring contest with a very narrow win for Vicky Sponge. Let's hope this is just the start of their rivalry, as these two novices put on an excellent show.

As it is: Vicky Sponge advances to the next stage of the try-outs to join her father's Sponge Dungeon gym this year, with her chance to join the FOOD FiGHT! and emulating his accomplishments drawing ever closer. A huge day for her in her journey to prove herself.

The big question is this: what next for Ring Doughnut?

Our thanks, as ever, go to our sponsors, these brave competitors, the fantastic staff and support here at the Sponge Dungeon for their hospitality, and, most importantly, to you, the fans watching at home. Good night.

BAZZ: Night? It's barely the afternoon.

Round 5:

Just Desserts

The clanking of the tin can on solid wood woke Ring Doughnut up.

Ring peeled himself out of bed and dragged his feet over to where the phone dangled, spurting into life then going limp for a second at a time. He wasn't sure when it had fallen off of the table. Wasn't sure about a few things.

He thought about cutting the string, chopping straight through the white fibres. Peace at last. No more noise. No need to tell anyone anything. He could just pretend the whole thing never happened.

He couldn't be bothered to find some scissors.

Ring held the can up, spoke into it. 'Hello. Over.'

'Ah, hello Mr Doughnut,' a cheery voice on the other end said. 'I've got a Mr Jam Tart on the other line for you. Do you accept? Over.'

'No. Over.'

'Putti- Oh. Erm, ok. It's just that... he's quite concerned, Mr Doughnut. Over.'

'Tell him I'm fine. Over and out.'

Ring dropped the tin can back to its position, hanging between the table and the floor, and sloped back to bed.

It was a good effort, blue gloves, but not enough. The words had been bouncing around his head for the last however many days since he'd got back. Since he'd returned home in failure.

He hadn't protested. Hadn't grovelled or moaned or disagreed.

He hadn't waited to hear any snide remarks from *her*, or thrown a vicious parting comment her way.

Ring Doughnut simply nodded and left.

After that, he'd dragged himself home. He walked the whole way but he couldn't recall any of it. Not even as much as which way he went or what time it was when he finally got back home; what he'd done other than flop into bed.

He knew he hadn't cried. Ring Doughnut had wanted to, but he stopped himself. Crying meant something, he'd determined, and he didn't want to admit that that something might have come to pass.

He hadn't thought about his grandfather either; or rather, he suppressed the thoughts, because if he didn't then he really would break down.

He stared at the ceiling, at the walls covered in the great and good of FOOD FiGHT!. The idols he was meant to emulate. To surpass.

You didn't even make it past the first round of the try-outs. Although he said it to himself, Ring heard it in *her* voice. Which was better than hearing the disappointment in *his* voice.

You won the last round but the other two went to your opponent because she landed the better shots. That was Fred Velvet's summary of the fight.

He had been kind, gentle. He'd been clear that Ring Doughnut was talented and encouraged him to come back next year. Again. Even after Ring had been so obnoxious, so arrogant to demand a match. The praise was hollow, the words still doomed him, even if they were delivered with sprinkles on top.

He didn't even know if he disagreed with the veteran trainer any more. The fight was a blur to him, a series of moments that he watched as though he was above the ring rather than in it. Most of what he saw was him being hit in the face, in the gut, being pushed back by astonishing punches from his opponent in the bright red gloves.

In those moments, he simply felt numb. Nothing. A weird listlessness. No push and no pull.

Other times, he saw himself as a flurry, a swirling blue and brown storm. He launched attack after attack after attack; saw her teetering on the brink. He saw the Sponge Dungeon in the background, the doors open and ready to welcome him.

In those moments, he felt an anger that burned his insides and threatened to melt him.

Keep going, get some bouts in. You'll win more than you lose, Velvet had said.

There was one moment that kept popping up. Lingered. A still image, a photograph. He saw it as a memory through his own eyes. Just the one. He was sure it had happened in the match, too. *She* was just off the ropes but her arms were down and her eyes were gazing off into the distance, and her feet tripped over each other as she lurched forwards, and Ring could see his right hand out ahead and his left arm low, and all he needed to do was to throw that uppercut.

That one good punch.

Why couldn't I do it?

'Why couldn't you do it?' He sighed.

'Why couldn't you just do it!?' He shouted.

He slammed his fists into his mattress and kicked his heels and he thought about screaming into his pillow. He screamed out, towards the ceiling, to the apartments above and to the rest of the Doughjo.

The can jangled against the table and the wall again.

Ring lay rigid in his bed, the back of his head pressed into the pillow, into the mattress.

'Go away,' he growled.

The tin can disobeyed him.

'Why can't they just leave me?' He grumbled, his teeth clenched so hard together they could crack.

The tin can pulsed again.

He grunted out of bed and thumped his feet loudly against the cardboard floor, cursing.

'What?' He shouted down the can.

There was no response.

'What? Over.' He repeated.

'There's a Mr Jam Tart on the line for you. Do you accept? Over.' The same voice - not as cheery or sweet as before, though.

'No. Tell him to leave me alone. Over.'

'Might I-'

'Over and out.'

Ring chucked the tin can at the wall, left a small dent in it. He'd have to pay to fix that. As if he wasn't paying enough for this place already.

'Brilliant, just brilliant,' he said, stomping back to his bed. 'Leave me alone. Just leave me alone and then I won't break anything and then I'll be ok. Just leave me alone!'

No sooner had he thrown his face into his pillow than the tin can was up to its old tricks again. Ring didn't wait this time. It had barely clanged once but he was over to the other side of the room in two paces with such force that he nearly crashed into the wall himself.

'Put him through,' he shouted. 'Put him through right now!'

'Mr Doughnut,' it was her again, and her voice quivered but held a neutral tone, 'I will not be spoken to like that. You might be having a bad day but there is no need to take it out on me. I am polite and respectful to you and the least I deserve is the same back.'

'I'm sorry,' Ring whispered, but she continued talking.

'I am putting you through to Mr Jam Tart now. Please hold the line. Over and out.'

'I'm sorry,' he said again, his voice stuck in his throat.

'You should be,' Jam replied, 'I've been trying to get hold of you for two days. What happened? Are you ok? It either went really well or... Well, yeah. How are you? Over.'

'I just don't want to talk, ok? Over.' Ring was still growling each word a single syllable at a time, but there was no force, no fire behind them as there had been when he sprinted over to the phone.

'Ring, come on. You left me in Calorifornia. Alone. I figured something bad must've happened. That's just not like you at all. Are you hurt? Over.'

'No, I'm fine. Over.' Ring ran his hands over his swollen face - the right cheek had blown up alongside his eye, and he had a couple of tears on his body around his sides, but he was otherwise fine. Just tired. Just angry.

You can sure take a punch - but you kept walking into them. My advice: work on your evasion, your body movement. Had Fred Velvet said that? Ring heard it in his voice but he wasn't sure now.

'Well then, I can tell you that you're a rubbish friend. I got up early to go with you, promised to document your story, to support you - and then you just went and left me? Not cool. Over.'

Is he joking? 'Well you obviously made it home or you wouldn't be able to bother me so much. Over.'

'Bother you? Ring, it's called caring. I hadn't heard from you for two days. Your mum tried too and they got nothing, said you wouldn't even answer the door. People worry. It's not bothering you-'

'It is bothering me. I said go away. The operator told you to go away and you kept ignoring her. It isn't my fault if you can't listen. Ov-
'

'Oh don't start. Don't start taking it out on me, Ring. So you failed your first ever try-out for the professional leagues. Big sad. You think you're going to make it if this is how you react to a minor setback? There will be other try-outs. There will b-
'

'-Stop, Jam. Stop. You don't get it. Over.'

'So explain then. Explain why it's so bad you would ditch me? Over.'

Ring didn't want to explain it. What was there to explain, anyway? He'd lost his first ever match and he'd blown his chance at joining the Sponge Dungeon. Blown his chance of getting onto the card of a FOOD FiGHT! event. Sure, there were other gyms, but he was already behind one boxer with no experience - so there must have been dozens of them who were better than him; who were getting even better under the expert tutelage of legends like "Drop-Dead" Fred Velvet; who would be picked for the big fight nights ahead of him. Even if he made his way through every single one of them, somehow, it would take so long that Cassius Cake would be comfortably retired.

He was never going to do what he set out to do. What he'd promised to do.

You were wrong. This was directed at Granddough. He thought about how disappointed his grandfather would have been with him. How he'd failed him. His face, wrinkled up in a frown, dulled eyes. The thought re-angered him, as did Jam pestering him on the other end of the line. His head was too full, full of thoughts he didn't want to keep having; full of comments he didn't want to hear, and disappointments he kept reliving again and again.

'Ring. Explain it. Over,' Jam said, curtly.

'I can't. I... I've blown my chance, Jam. I'm never going to win the FOOD FiGHT! Championship now. I'm never going to have my match with the "King", or meet Walter Waffle, or box at the Cake Stand Stadium. I'm never going to be a boxer. It's over. Over.'

'Ring, buddy,' Jam said, his voice bubbly, 'I don't want to sound like a bad friend here but: did you actually think you were going to become the champion? Like, I know it's your dream and all, and I know that you and your granddad used to talk about it, but I thought it was more of a "Oh yeah, it would be cool to be champion" rather than a

"This is my destiny" kind of deal. Like it was a long-shot but if you were lucky then maybe? Sorry. Do you get what I mean? Over.'

Jaw clenched. Eyes dry, staring at the dent in the wall he'd made earlier. One fist balled up, the other trying its best to crush the tin can.

'Sorry, that didn't come out very well. I can hear it now. Sorry, Ring. I just mean like nobody wins the championship this young. You've never even had a match before. So it was a lot of pressure on your first try-out. But you could join another gym and work your way up, rather than starting at the top. You could still get there eventually. Actually, it's all good material for the article, *heh*. Another twist in the story of Ring Doughnut's rise to the top.' He paused. 'Are you still there? Over.'

'Oh well, if we're talking about things that will never happen, that article is a great place to start. Even if I beat Cassius Cake in a single punch in the first round, you'd still never be able to finish it or get it published. That's why you can't comprehend someone trying to be something, because you never stick with anything. You latch onto a passing fad and never get anywhere.'

'Hold on, Ring.'

'I'm not done. How many times have you tried to be something and then given up? How many dreams have you had in the last month? In the last week? I've had one dream and I put everything into it. Granddough put everything into it. But I failed. I failed. That isn't a familiar feeling for me. I don't fail every single day and move onto the next thing. I actually care, an-'

'Look, I said I was sorry. Why don't we call it even? You left me at Calorifornia, I messed up here. Truce? What d'ya say, equal? Over.'

'We're not equal, though, Jam. Maybe that's the problem. Instead of hanging out with others who want to be the best and who know they can be, I've been limiting myself. Hanging out with folks who are happy to settle for a middling life, who think being a nobody is wo-'

'Right, shut up now. You're right: we're not equal. You don't get to talk to me like that, even if you're sad and angry. I only wanted to check that you were ok. I didn't sign up for the rest of this.' Jam paused, but not long enough for Ring to start up again. 'You want to know what failing looks like? It's this, Ring. Next time you need some company for a try-out, don't bother asking me. See you around. Over and out.'

The line went dead.

Ring had never heard Jam speak like that before. The flatness. The hurt.

I failed.

You were wrong about me.

'Brilliant, nice one, Ring,' he shouted at himself, suddenly awash with regret and embarrassment and an intense, burning fury.

He hurled the can at the wall and it lodged itself into the cardboard.

The next few minutes were a frenzy.

Sat on the floor amongst ripped posters, with the punchbag turned on its side and his bed now looking lop-sided, Ring Doughnut realised he had to get out the apartment.

'Idiot,' he remonstrated.

Why are you being like this? Granddough wouldn't have wanted this.

'If it makes you act like this, is it worth it?' He asked.

Only one poster remained intact: the "Undoughsputed" fight, with "King" Cassius Cake on the left and "Marvellous" Marvin Bagel on the right, the two staring at each other with that word between them. Their names written in huge type in the centre of the poster, beneath the FOOD FiGHT! logo in its older, original style, before they rebranded a couple of years later. At the bottom of the poster were names of other boxers who had matches that night, names that he couldn't read from his position slumped against the door. They were still a part of history, though, and Ring

Doughnut had researched them all over the years. Some had gone on to have decent careers, but most sort of faded away. Unknowns.

Did Cassius Cake know that this match would be the first time he was ever truly tested? He looked so at ease on the poster. Confident, borderline carefree. He was about to box against the BUN FiGHT! Champion, box on behalf of all of those who would never have had the opportunity without "Iced" Finger Bun and his call for equality. Box for the title of "Undisputed", the very right to call himself the best of the best in the Doughjo.

Marvin Bagel looked angry, looked like he felt the weight of history.

But Cassius Cake just had something else. He held an assuredness that he would win, an easiness about the whole thing.

'Why don't I have that?' Ring asked.

Beneath the poster, he spotted his gloves. They lay apart from when he'd kicked them, but the royal blue stood out against the brown and beige of the rest of the room.

Ring shuffled over on his backside and picked them up, held them in his hands. He studied the "Recipe for Success" branding on the wrist straps, the quality of the pink laces. He saw the scuff marks from the fight he'd lost, felt the padding inside was a little less puffy than it had been when he'd bought them.

It was a good effort, blue gloves, but not enough.

He looked around the room. At least his mum couldn't say it had no personality now. The only problem being that the personality it had taken on wasn't one that she'd like. It wasn't one that Ring liked, either.

He placed the gloves together on the floor and set about tidying up the torn scraps of paper.

He pulled the tin can out of the dent he'd created in the wall. Put the table back on its legs. Placed the tin can in position, so it wasn't just hanging from the ceiling.

Ring heaved his punchbag back upright with a great deal of effort, and he looked at the bed - which he wouldn't be able to fix - and straightened out the duvet and pillows.

The room wasn't perfect, but it was better. It looked messy rather than angry.

'Right, last thing, then get some fresh air,' he said to himself, walking over to the poster.

It was warm and bright outside Ring's apartment, and the Doughjo was bustling with movement. It must have been mid-afternoon. The normality of it all made his head hurt.

Jam said it had been two days, Ring realised.

He wondered how long we would have stayed inside if not for his friend's insistence on talking to him.

Ring took a deep breath and walked towards the stairs, his bag bouncing gently on his back as he did so. Truthfully, he was still upset, but it was only upset now. The anger had subsided and it was more a feeling of regret and disappointment.

You didn't even make it past the first round of try-outs.

Alright so maybe it wasn't *just* upset. Maybe there was still some anger as the memory came back to him. No, not a memory, that never happened, those words were never spoken; but he was sure *she* would've said that to him if she'd had the chance. *She* probably thought it, was probably reliving that same moment herself now, giggling and gleeful at her career being all lined up; at the training programme her dad made for her and the hand-picked opponents to improve her record.

Ring Doughnut wouldn't be so lucky. He'd have to learn the hard way. He'd have to learn by being thumped in the face by boxers with heaps of experience and fights under their belt. He'd be at risk of a bad match-up; at risk of a couple of rogue losses to dodgy judges or too-cautious referees.

If he could be bothered. It all felt so far away.

And he'd always have that loss on his record to

her. An asterisk.

How was he meant to reach the top when he was starting from so much further down? Not even Cassius Cake had had to climb from the very bottom tier. He'd been spotted early and trained by Victor Sponge himself.

Thudding down the stairs, his feet slapping against the cold metal, the sound echoing up to the top shelf where he started, he caught a couple of looks from others heading up past him but nobody said anything. Nobody reached out or asked to comfort him. Good, he didn't deserve it. Not after how he'd acted to Jam, and to the line operator who he'd shouted at.

What am I doing? Ring suddenly felt the urge to go back to bed. He was one flight away from the shop floor and the fresh air, but his mood had soured. Again. He just couldn't stop hearing *her* voice and seeing *her* stupid grin.

You didn't even make it past the first rou-

'Oh, well, fancy seeing you here.'

Ring looked at the open door to the stairwell, saw the familiar sight of his sister, Sugar, stood there. She was a ball doughnut - no hole in the middle - and she was the younger sibling by a couple of years. She wore a bored expression most of the time, but she gave away genuine surprise and a flicker of a smile in this moment. She changed her hairstyle every day, and today it was blackcurrant jam, styled in a short quiff.

'Mum's been worried about you. Your friend kept calling her,' Sugar said.

'What's his problem?' Ring grunted. 'Well, you've seen me now. Tell her I'm fine.'

'Where are you going?' Sugar asked.

Ring was climbing the stairs. He didn't want an argument but he felt argumentative, like all he could say would come across as accusatory and inflammatory.

'Oi, bro. Come on. Talk.'

'Not in the mood. Besides, when do we ever talk?'

Sugar started climbing the stairs. 'When I need some new material. Come on. What happened at that try-out?'

'I failed. Alright? It's over.' Had he said that out loud before? It felt uneasy. A weight had been lifted, and another had been added immediately. Was he lighter than before? Did he mean it?

'So where were you going with your gym bag, then? Is this some weird cover-up they have you do at the Sponge Down?' Sugar smiled, her big eyes twinkled.

'You know it's not called that. I really don't want to chat. I'm fine, I'll be fine. I'm just not totally fine right now, ok?'

'Ring.' Sugar's face held a dead-pan expression, a raised eyebrow.

'Sugar.' Ring tried to return the favour but his swollen eye made it impossible. He felt tears in his eyes.

'Ring.' Softness now, a gentle tone. A half-smile.

'It's just been- Eurg.' A single tear managed to escape and roll down his cheek, his right-hand side, leaving a trail down his body. He wiped his eye, shook his head. 'I'm honestly fine. Will be fine.' He managed a smile that felt as unnatural as anything he'd ever done in his entire life.

'Well, how about this then: why don't you come back home and tell Mum yourself? Ah, wait for me to finish. Come back home and tell Mum yourself - and then you can help out with a couple of jobs around the place. Otherwise, she'll do them all herself and we all know how that ends up. Remember the wonky wall?'

Ring smiled. The wonky wall was an entire wall in their lounge covered in family photos - not a single one of which was hung up level. What was even weirder was they all had different angles, but Ring's Mum insisted that they were all fine.

'So come back, do some odd jobs so that I don't have to, tell Mum you're fine. She'll probably moan about me as well, so that'll be a bonus. Sounds like a good way to spend the afternoon, right?'

Ring was about to protest, but Sugar had already linked her arm in his and was pulling him back down the stairs. He didn't resist, allowed himself to be dragged out onto the wooden shop floor, the planks toasty under his feet; the place busier than it had looked from the top shelf. Folks shopping, chatting, travelling, working.

'So, what were you planning to do before I bumped into you?' Sugar asked.

'I had a few things to get rid of,' he replied. 'Where were you going?'

'The Sponge Bath.' Sugar winked, jabbed him in a painful spot on his side that drew a wince. 'I have to get revenge for the honour of my family.'

Ring didn't laugh, stopped still. 'Look, I'll come and visit and chat but I don't want to talk about what happened or else I'll go home. Ok?'

'Woah, sorry. Sorry. That's it, I promise.'

Ring started walking again, irritated. Unsure at who the bulk of the irritation was directed at.

'How's it all going with Mum?' Ring asked.

'Not great. One guest at the moment, here for just the one night,' Sugar sighed. 'Probably don't ask Mum about it though. She'll say it's fine.'

'So that's where I get it from.' Ring allowed himself the smallest of smiles.

'Honestly, I swear I'm adopted,' Sugar laughed.

You'd never know that the business was struggling from the outside.

A four-storey high building with a glossy white exterior and exquisite round windows made from the bases of unused jam jars, immaculately clean so that it sparkled with the little afternoon sunshine it received down here on the shop floor. Grey steps led up to a revolving glass door, edged with gold. Ring wondered where the porter was today; usually someone would be stood in a tailored suit and top hat, ready to welcome guests in.

The sign above the front door was written in delicate black calligraphy: Doughchester Hotel.

'Has Mum had that redone?' Ring asked.

'Good eyes. She said it made it look classier. Make sure you let her know you like it,' Sugar replied.

'I didn't say that.'

'I didn't say you had to mean it, either.'

Sugar took the steps in two great leaps, whereas Ring climbed more slowly on account of a stabbing pain in his side. He tried not to wince but the aching had ratcheted up as he'd been chaperoned back to the family hotel in a half-walk, half-drag.

Ring waddled slowly around with the revolving door until he was stood in the foyer.

Soft, plump furniture - intentionally mismatched in reds and golds and blacks and whites - alongside family photographs, to give the place a cosy feel. Thrown in to the mix was the odd painting or two on canvas, one of his mum's favourite hobbies, that would inevitably resemble whatever it wasn't meant to. There were three different desks, only differentiated by the fact that one had the word 'Reception' on the front in the old, thick stencilled style of font that used to adorn the hotel's frontage.

He could hear his mum clanging about from under the desk, dragging around a tin can whilst trying to find something she'd carefully filed away in her system. The white string boinged above her as the sound of paper spreading all over the floor filled the room.

It was a good job something filled the silence, anyway. The foyer was empty. No staff, no people waiting to check-in or check-out, or take on advice about entertainment in Alacrumba. Just furniture and photographs.

'Just the one night? Why not make it two or three? You know, the back of the Doughjo is really not as bad as it once was,' Ring's mum said with a weird titter. 'No? Ok, just the one night. Name of Madeleine. Ok, well I'll see you in a couple of weeks. Goodbye.'

Without emerging from beneath the desk, Ring's mum shouted: 'I'll be with you in a moment!'

Ring and Sugar looked at each other. Sugar held a finger to her mouth.

'It's only me, Mum,' she said.

'Oh, good. Where have you put the guest reservation list? I've booked a room that we might not have. You have to start following my system, Sugar, or this whole thing will fall apart. Oh, and another thing: I need you to help tidy the rooms tomorrow.'

Sugar leaned over the desk, pulled a sheet of paper from one of the thick wooden drawers. Knocked on the top of the desk, which drew a sort of yelp from their mum. Ring found the noise so peculiar he struggled not to laugh.

'Oh, well, it should've gone in this box down here. You can tidy this up for me, my knees are sore from all this rummaging around. I need to go and soak them.'

'Eurg,' Sugar sighed, 'sure. Also, Ring's here.'

'What?'

'Sugar? I thought we were going to do something funny,' Ring said, smiling awkwardly.

'That was before I got lumped with all the chores. See? Mum's favourite over there, leaves and never has to help out any more.' Sugar winked at him, held out an arm to help her mum stand up straight.

Mum was also a ball doughnut, just like Sugar, but she was smaller and she wore thick-rimmed black spectacles high on her face. A two-piece white suit didn't seem to suit her at all, although the same couldn't be said for her signature white pearl necklace. Ring had never seen her without it. She didn't look as plump as she used to, and she was a little bit hunched, a little bit shorter. More creases had appeared around her eyes, and her glaze was cracked, dry.

How long had it been since he'd seen her? They didn't even live that far apart - but coming home always ended the same way, so he never really bothered to come home.

'Hey Mum,' he waved.

Mum burst from behind the desk and gave him a great big squeeze, her head not even up to his chin.

'Oh, it is so nice to have my son home,' she said, 'we both miss you a great deal.'

Ring winced as she tightened her grip. This caused her to shoot a look up and actually see his swollen face and battered body.

'What happened?' She asked.

'He doesn't want to talk about it,' Sugar said quickly, scooping up papers and dumping them in a box.

'I don't care about that,' Mum replied, 'I'm his mother. I need to know. What happened? Tell me you're not going to box anymore.'

Ring had never been good at deflecting this sort of question. Granddough had always been able to laugh it off or distract her with another topic, but Ring felt prickly and annoyed. He tended to clam up and grunt answers.

'I had a try-out. Didn't make it,' he said.

'So that's it? You're done with boxing now? You could move ho-'

'-Mum, don't start. Can't we just have a normal conversation?' He shrugged out of the embrace but avoided looking at her, lest he see she was upset.

'Well, a normal conversation would involve me asking how you are but I can see you are not very well at all.' She poked at his side, and he winced again.

'It's still polite to ask.'

'We're family. We don't need to be polite.'

Sugar laughed, caught a glare from both of them and disappeared back under the desk to grapple with another box.

'How are things here? I saw the new sign out front,' Ring said. 'Very... new.' Ring tried to find the right word but failed, not that his mum seemed to mind.

'It's classy, isn't it? Shows we're a high-level

establishment.'

'Yes, very classy.' *Classy! That's what Sugar had told him to say.*

'It should attract a bit more passing trade,' she smiled. 'So, what brings you back here then?'

'Me,' Sugar shouted, taking a box through the door to the office that was behind the desk.

'Oh, so you're not here to return my calls in person? Your friend Jam called here so many times, too. I came up to your apartment but there was no answer.'

'Rough couple of days,' Ring said. He was irritated but trying not to show it. When he was younger, he'd got on so well with his mum. They could talk for hours and hours, share every detail. Now, though, it always felt so staged. A theatre between them. Ring cared, and he knew she cared. But something about the conversation always felt slightly off, as though both of them were looking for the earliest exit. Was that happening now? Or was he just hoping it was so he could go back to his broken bed and wallow a bit longer?

He wouldn't ever tell his sister, but he preferred it when Sugar was around. It gave them a common enemy.

'Hmmm, "rough couple of days". Hmmm.' Ring's mum was shuffling back to the desk.

'What?'

'What "what"?'

'What is it you aren't saying, Mum?'

'You said not to talk about it, so I'm not.'

'This was stupid. Coming back here was so stupid. Tell Sugar I said bye.'

'Wait, Ring, wait,' his mum called, but Ring was in no mood to wait.

He turned on his heels and marched to the revolving door, ignoring his mum's pleas and the sound of her slip-ons slapping against the polished floor. He had come out for fresh air and instead was being met by dated arguments and stale relationships. He didn't need this. Any of it. He was trying to keep his cool and trying to not let it all bother him, but all these jabs and comments from everyone. How did they not know how important this was to him? How important it had been to Granddough, too? Ring couldn't believe everyone was so blind to his ambitions and his dreams.

He stopped before he reached the door, turned to face her. Sugar was in the office doorway, and she shook her head. Ring ignored her.

'You know what's in this bag, Mum? It's my boxing stuff. I was coming out today to give it away. But maybe you should have it? Then you can sell it, actually make a bit of profit here for once.' That one hurt her, he could tell. He threw the bag on the floor with a thud.

'Mum doesn't want you to quit, do you, Mum?' Sugar offered, stepping forwards.

'Oh, come on! That's all she has ever wanted. She hated that I boxed. Well, guess what? I can't any more. I failed. All those days and weeks training with Granddough, and I wasn't good enough to get past the first round. I failed him. And now every time I look at the gloves or the posters or any of it, I only see the time he wasted trying to turn me into a somebody. And I won't ever get to make it right because he isn't here anymore. So there, have the stuff. Granddough was wrong about me and you were right all along.' Ring pushed through the door before the tears could escape. He wouldn't let them see him cry.

Granddough would be so ashamed, he said to himself, and anger and disappointment awakened simultaneously. Ring didn't know if he'd explode in a rage or if he'd deflate into a puddle if he stayed, if he heard what his mum had to say.

Didn't want to find out, either.

He'd barely cleared the last step when Sugar came storming out after him.

'What was that, Ring? Mum's in tears. Why couldn't you two just play nicely for once?' She asked the question loud enough that a few passers-by turned to look at them.

'She always does the same thing though! She literally always nags me about quitting boxing. Now I tell her I have quit and she's crying? Well, that isn't my problem.' He turned to go, felt a hand on his shoulder. He shrugged it off, so Sugar ran around in front of him.

'Just go back and talk to her.'

'No. It's always the same. It's a waste of time.'

'So is you running around shouting at everyone!' She scoffed, adding, 'Jam told me you weren't in a good way.'

Ring tried to get past her but she side-stepped, blocking him each time.

'You're not going anywhere until you go back and have a proper talk with Mum. I mean it. You two need to sort this out,' Sugar warned him.

'I'm going home. I'm not wasting another moment of my life in there.'

Blocked again. 'Ring. Do it for me, then.'

Ring turned around to walk the other way but Sugar scuttled in front of him. He glanced up and saw his mum behind the revolving door like a ghost. Looked away again.

'This isn't what Granddough would've wanted. He hated when you two argued.'

'Don't you dare,' Ring growled.

'You know we all loved him too, Ring? Mum would love to talk to you about him. She knew him before we did. There's loads we don't know about him. Maybe you could ask her about him? Please, Ring. It's not been easy since we lost him and you moved out.'

'Just leave me alone already,' Ring said, his eyes stinging. Heart sore. He wanted to get home now. He shoved Sugar out the way.

Regretted it immediately.

It wasn't a heavy shove. It wasn't a powerful shove. It wasn't a shove with any malice behind it.

However, as he watched Sugar fall in slow motion, the world around Ring seemed to fade to black, the aisle fell silent. It was as though nobody else was moving.

Her feet had tangled up, and she whacked her head on the wooden shop floor with a nasty crash. There was a rip above her eye and jam the colour of new boxing gloves oozed out, a trail down her cheek and her side. She looked him dead in the eye, and he couldn't turn away. She cursed, and she cursed again, and she patted the ooze as it progressed down her face and she cursed once more, louder and with more venom.

'Great going. Idiot.' Sugar winced, pinching at the tear above her eye. It wasn't that deep or wide, but it must've just been in the wrong place.

Ring didn't know what to say.

What could he say?

She's ok, Ring. Just go, he told himself, but it didn't feel right. That wasn't him saying it. Not the real him. That was whatever he'd been the last few days. The husk that he'd become after the events at the Sponge Dungeon.

'Oh, my goodness, are you ok, ma'am?' A small snickerdoodle gasped, sucking air between her teeth when she saw the wound. She shot Ring a dirty look.

Ring was frozen, staring at his fallen sister. His mouth gaped but nothing came out. He hadn't meant to push her over, just to get her out of his way. The snickerdoodle said something to him but he didn't really hear them, didn't process their voice.

What had happened to him? Had boxing really taken over his life to the extent that he'd make his mum cry and he'd hurt his sister? Not just in the same day, but within the same minute. No, to blame boxing would be an easy way out. This was Ring's fault. He'd let his frustration, his disappointment, and his anger get the better of him. This wasn't the behaviour of the heir to the throne - but, more importantly, it wasn't the behaviour of a friend, or a son, or a brother.

Or a grandson.

You didn't even make it past the first round. Not Vicky Sponge's voice this time but his grandfather's. The same encouraging, enthusiastic tone he heard when he was winning matches against the legends of the sport from the comfort of his bedroom. Not accusatory, but smiling, familiar. A shrug and an easy grin. Warm. *You didn't even make it past the first round. So what? You're still a champion, Ringo!*

Ring took a step forward, crouched in towards his sister who was being advised not to move by the snickerdoodle.

'Sugar, I'm really sor-'

Ring suddenly felt his body crushing into the thick, black cardboard facade of the building next door to the Doughchester Hotel. His right shoulder hit awkwardly and he felt a shooting pain down through his fingers. When he turned his head, he saw the thump had come from the largest cinnamon bun he'd ever seen. The thick, caramel-coloured icing on its body had a Ring-shaped imprint in it.

'Hey, watch it,' Ring spluttered, his words iced with pain.

'You think it's good to go around hitting folks in the street, do you? You gonna hit me, huh?' The cinnamon bun advanced towards Ring, puffing out his front, his thick arms. Ring was only two-thirds as tall as him at best, and he would bet he was giving up a lot of weight.

'He's ok, he's my brother,' Sugar said weakly from the floor. 'It was an accident.'

'Nope, not ok. Not ok at all.' The cinnamon bun started pounding his right fist into his left palm repeatedly. 'Gonna have to teach him a lesson.'

'Excuse me, stop. I said it's fine.' Ring could see Sugar being helped to her feet by the snickerdoodle, one arm around the small cookie's shoulders. She looked bad, there was no way around it. That was a mean looking cut.

Cinnamon turned around, 'What about when he does it to someone else's sister? Or their mum? Or their grandma? Where I'm from, these lessons need to be taught the right way.'

'Look, I don't want a fi-' Ring was interrupted by a huge swinging hook. He managed to duck down, heard the gasps, heard Sugar shriek.

'Stop! I told you to stop!' She cried.

Ring held his palms up, a gesture of non-combat. Ignored as another wild punch flew past him. Ring kept backing up, stammered a few different reasons to stop, all while Sugar was wailing, asking for help from passers-by. Ring couldn't see if the cinnamon bun had any friends - he hoped he didn't - and he felt his head pulsing and his eyes dry out, his arms start to tingle. The pain across his body numbed slightly, and he was breathing faster.

A single high-pitch drone, an unbroken note, was all that filled his ears. He couldn't even make out what the cinnamon bun was saying, stood still and wide, arms flexing. A wicked grin fixed on that fat face. He dived at Ring, throwing an overhand that Ring managed to skittle out of the way of; instinctively threw a counter-punch that caught the bun between the eyes.

The small crowd gathered gasped.

'Now you're in trouble,' the cinnamon bun growled.

Keep going, get some bouts in.

Ring decided he didn't really have another option.

Ring moved into his familiar stance, side on, right hand out front, left hand waiting to be unleashed. He was on the balls of his feet, ready to move, ready to dart back from danger or forward into an opportunity to strike.

One good punch, he advised himself - and it would have to be.

Cinnamon was big and slow, but he had power. Ring would have to avoid getting hit, and see what he could do on the counter. His first riposte had stung, at least, so there was hope.

His aches and pains screamed as he waited for

the next attack. His left arm didn't feel good and his body was still sore and his eye, his swollen eye, made seeing things just that little bit more difficult.

'Come here,' grunted Cinnamon, another looping overhand punch missing.

Ring fired back a quick jab with his right hand. It came back covered in the thick icing, seemingly had no effect on his giant opponent. Hurt his fist, too. This is why he'd worn gloves at the try-out.

He moved forward again, picked off another two jabs towards the face, then skipped back. A good tempo, good momentum. He had this.

Ring ducked another punch, and was too quick for the follow-up. He could see Cinnamon getting angrier, although the bigger fighter had a big grin on his face.

One good punch.

The longer it went on, the more risk there was for Ring. He landed another couple of punches to the body and the face, and, confident in his ability to hit his opponent whenever and wherever he wanted, he prepared for a finale. His finishing manoeuvre.

Cinnamon threw another wild haymaker and Ring slipped through. Jab, jab, left-hook. Clean connection. Low in the hips, rotating upward to hit an uppercut.

Not just any uppercut either. *His* uppercut: the

Glazed Over.

Ring threw his body weight into it and- *Ouch!* His right arm was too painful, he pulled the shot, caught Cinnamon on the chin - but without any great force.

The big dumb grin on his opponent's face was broad and hungry.

Ring was too close to get away.

He took a heavy knee into the mid-section and choked, unable to remember how to breathe. Unable to protest that Cinnamon had used his knee. That wasn't legal!

Then a follow-up to the face which hurt worse than anything he'd ever felt before. His eyes were full of tears and he could only see outlines, fuzzy objects. A thumping in his head. He staggered back and put up a flimsy guard, threw a weird half-punch with his right hand.

Cinnamon caught his arm and twisted it behind his back. Yanked it back, as though he was trying to rip it off. Ring wailed. He forgot how to say words, how to express the agony he felt.

He was being pushed forward until his face crunched into the building he'd been thumped into earlier. A heavy hand thudded his face into it again. Once more, before Ring managed to wriggle free.

'Oh, you're still standing? You want some more?' Cinnamon shouted.

Ring groggily rotated. Only now did he notice the crowd that had gathered. He couldn't make out features and faces very easily, but he could see at least two dozen citizens stood watching, gasping, muttering. A high-pitched whine in his ears.

Still, that sage advice: *one good punch.*

Ring decided to try an inverted "Glazed Over". He'd use his right hand. He had one shot, he knew that much. Even attempting it would probably wind the big brute up more, but he couldn't just let himself get beaten up, and Ring sensed his opponent was just getting warmed up.

Ring moved into position as best he could, left hand now leading. He tried to focus on the mass moving towards him, tried to locate the chin, or at least the face.

Got it.

He threw all his weight into the punch.

It connected. Clean.

Rocked Cinnamon backwards, scrambling a bit. Ring could hear the crowd gasp in unison, even thought he heard a cheer. Ring wanted to move forwards, spurred on by the momentum, but his body was heavy and slow, and his steps weren't co-ordinated.

Cinnamon charged him, tackled him around the legs. Ring crashed to the exposed wooden floorboards. Cinnamon was mounted above him, right fist held high, a shadow against the fluorescent lights.

'You're done now!' Cinnamon shouted, bringing the fist down.

Ring closed his eyes.

But he didn't feel a thing.

Had he been punched so hard that he'd lost consciousness? Had he been punched so hard that his expiry date had been brought forward? That he'd gone to meet his baker?

There were noises, though. Not noises. Voices.

He could still feel the heat of the floorboards.

Somehow, he was sure he could smell the sawdust and the fresh bread from Breadinburgh, even though he was all the way at the back of the shop.

He opened his eyes.

A shadow against the light was there still, but it was not a huge fist any more. It was a face. A face with a brown moustache and thick, square glasses. A face with a brown fedora on its head. A round face with a round body and a brown sports jacket.

A face with a voice that said, 'You ok, kid?'

A face that was being thanked and hugged by Ring's mum. A face that helped Ring to his feet, holding him upright, waving off the onlookers, and took him back into the Doughchester Hotel and eased him on to a chair in the office behind the reception desk.

A face that said something to Ring's mum, and handed her a small rectangle of cardboard.

A face that left the room as Ring fell into a deep sleep.

Twelve Days Later

For the first three days after the brawl in the aisle, Ring slept, because not sleeping meant he had to acknowledge just how much pain he was in. Chunks and scrapes and tears all over. He knew he still had all his limbs because each of them hurt so badly that moving them caused him to wince and swear.

He vaguely remembered his mum and his sister coming in to see him, but what they said, what they did… Nope, nothing.

Someone had been crying, hadn't they?

Where was he? The room felt familiar but with his eyes swollen this badly he could barely make out anything in the blurs.

Just sleep it off, Ring.

He took his own advice.

Day four sucked. It still hurt to move and his sight was only marginally better.

Was this what it was like after every fight? Ring didn't fancy that. Days of pain all for thirty or so minutes of glory. It didn't seem worth it. He thought of how often the "King" must have experienced this.

You need to work on taking less hits. He smiled, recalling the advice of "Drop-Dead" Fred Velvet on that fateful day. That stung as well, re-opened a cut on his lip.

If only he'd actioned that advice a bit sooner.

Ring had realised he was in the Doughchester Hotel, at least. Not that he could get up and explore, because sitting up made him feel dizzy and nauseous. Still, it felt comforting to hear his mum and sister walking about, talking to each other before heading down for work. Laughing. Ring didn't always associate humour with the two of them, but they got on so well.

Maybe I was the problem all along? He thought.

Idle thoughts drifted off to the bottle green chairs in Granddough's house. The day after the "Undoughsputed" fight, the story of his retirement bout with the "King". The way Granddough told it, the match wasn't anything special. A hard twelve round contest fought in front of a decent-sized crowd that Cake won via split decision - an unpopular result with the crowd, but not unfair. Cake moved on to a number one contender's fight after that; and Granddough moved on to a life outside of the ropes.

It was one of the only professional bouts Cassius Cake had ever fought that Ring Doughnut hadn't seen. He found it difficult to imagine the two of them throwing punches at each other. In his head, Granddough was still wrinkled and hunched over, in his white vest, holding a walking cane despite the fact he was in his boxing gloves; while Cassius Cake was the imperious champion he'd always known.

I wonder who the judge was that thought Granddough won, he thought.

Ring made a note of the thought and rolled onto his side with a little yelp, trying to stave off another bout of dizziness.

On the fifth day, he realised he was in his old room at the top of the Doughchester Hotel. Where the walls were once adorned with pictures and posters, they were now bare and baby blue, slightly lighter where the old glossy prints had been. A patchwork feel. One wall was covered entirely in cardboard boxes with his name written in large capital letters on the side. Ring went to open one but found lifting it was too much. He took a seat at his old desk and pulled out one of the light wooden drawers. His old notebook was still there. A dirty red front page and tatty edges sticking out the side.

'Strategies and tactics by Ring Doughnut,' he muttered, a half-smile on his face.

He scanned them briefly. The first third of the book was dedicated to Cassius Cake, specifically his early career. The notes on the "Undoughsputed" fight were extensive, particularly a section around how "Marvellous" Marvin Bagel should have lost in the sixth round. Having watched the fight back numerous times since then, Ring Doughnut still held that sentiment. The referee had saved him.

He wanted to keep reading but his head pulsated and he felt like his eyes were bulging so much they might fall off of his face, so he put the notebook on the side, closed the drawer, and returned to bed.

Still, he felt good. It was progress, good to get out of bed. A waft of fresh air rolled over him and he realised someone had opened the window. He briefly thought about calling out to see if anyone was in, but figured it would be best to wait until he felt refreshed. A little snooze first, then a chat.

Just for a bit, he told himself.

A bit turned out to be until the evening of the sixth day, when he actually felt incredibly well, all things considered.

His eyes weren't so heavy and his mouth wasn't so swollen, and even his body wasn't spiking with soreness, although there was a constant buzz of pain under the surface.

He managed to get up and drag himself out of his room, propped up against the walls of the corridor, each step surprisingly not as painful as he was expecting despite his unsteadiness.

The home he grew up in was in fact just the top, top floor of the Doughchester Hotel. A secret fifth floor in the loft. Whereas other floors had an elevator to take guests almost to their door, the fifth floor required the use of a set of stairs that was accessed through a 'staff only' cupboard on the fourth floor. Why it had to be kept so secret, Ring had no idea - but Mum was insistent that no guests knew they lived just upstairs.

The fifth floor had three bedrooms - for Ring, Sugar, and their mum, respectively - and a lounge area, which Ring was shuffling towards now. This was usually decorated with whatever Ring's mum had decided not to use in the rest of the hotel, so it was often an assortment of odd pieces of furniture that didn't go together - a gold-leaf throne with red cushioning in one corner; a plastic orange cube that acted as a side-table right next to it. The wonky wall provided the backdrop, making it appear to Ring as though the whole room might just slide away at any given moment.

'Oh! Ring, it's you,' Sugar whispered. She was holding a rolling pin.

'Everything ok?' Ring asked, also whispering.

'I forgot you were here. I thought you were a burglar,' she grinned, lowering the weapon. 'It's literally the middle of the night.'

'Sorry, I just woke up. Guess I'll head back to bed.'

Sugar yawned, shook her head. She rubbed at her eyes and Ring only then noticed the wound on her head. It wasn't oozing anymore, but it looked painful. He winced.

'I'm so sorry. How is it?' he said. 'I didn't mean for it to happen. I was jus-'

'You've already said sorry like a million times already. Remember? Apology accepted. I'm sorry too.' She held out her fist and he bumped it with his own. 'It barely even hurts now, anyway. You're the one who looks worse for wear.'

'Still, I just wish I hadn't got so caught up. Anyway, I'll let you get back to bed.' Ring could tell

Sugar was tired, fighting back heavy eyes.

'You sure? I can stay up if you want some company. For a bit.'

'Yeah, I'm sure,' Ring lied. 'Go get some sleep.'

'We should catch-up properly tomorrow,' she smiled, turning away. 'Oh, also: Mum's really happy you're here, so make sure you make the most of that, ok?'

'She is?'

'Yeah, loves having you back. You two had a good chat the other day, or so I'm told.'

'We did?' Ring didn't remember that at all. 'Did she say what about?'

'Nope, just that she's happy to have you back. Maybe don't say you're feeling too good, though. You know what she's like: she'll have you working a shift or two downstairs.'

'Ha, I'll make sure I limp a bit then,' Ring grinned.

'How are you feeling, though?' Sugar said, stifling another yawn.

Ring yawned in response, 'Oh, pretty good right now. Pretty good.'

'That's good. Yeah, anyway, if you're sure you don't want some company now then I guess I'll go back to bed.'

Ring smiled, 'Night, sis.'

'Sweet dreams,' she whispered sleepily.

They did catch-up on day seven, and Ring found out that Sugar was seeing someone. Nothing serious. Well, not nothing - but not yet serious enough to announce any details, according to his sister. But serious enough to know it could be that serious in the future.

Otherwise, nothing much had changed. She was still working at the hotel, still unsure where her life was going to take her beyond that, or even if it needed to. Running a hotel wasn't easy but she was good at it, and she knew it so well now. She just wished that more of the fine folks of the Doughjo wanted to stay there. Ring admired how she was so confident, surrounded by pools of uncertainty.

Ring also spent some time with his mum. She did not once mention anything about the fight, kept her focus on idle things like the hotel, jobs to be done around the place, about how important it was that Sugar had her brother to rely on.

'It's not easy running the hotel alone and I won't be here forever,' she said.

'Don't talk like that, Mum.'

'Well it's true. Sugar is so good at keeping this place going, I'd be lost without her - but she'll need help.'

And who would you like to help her? Ring didn't say.

He left a silence that he knew his mum would fill, and she moved on to talking about old classmates of his that he no longer kept in touch with or never really liked in the first place.

As his mind idled away from the conversation, only intermittently reminding him to make some noise as though he was listening, Ring found himself wondering if it really would be so bad if he was to come back here. Not to live, necessarily. The short distance between them was good for everyone. Good to have that breathing space. But to help out. To have a career and a purpose here. He could help bring the good times back. He didn't know how just yet, but once he'd spent a bit of time here, he was sure he'd have a good idea.

Or maybe Sugar already had a great idea, and he could give her the space to think about innovation a bit more without needing to do a myriad of other tasks. He could do the filing, the fixing. The administration. Give Sugar time to redecorate the rooms or pick out a new font for the shop floor facade.

'Do you remember the Bakewells? Well, Cherry got into building work and does a bit of everything now. They always said she'd end up as a high-flyer in the Central Biscuit District with her smarts. Not so smug now. Not that there's anything wrong with building work, mind you.

We could use her around here, I think.'

'Wow, yeah. Good for Cherry,' Ring nodded.

'You could do that. Maybe you could do an apprenticeship with her. I'm sure she's a very good teacher. Always very likeable as well.'

'Maybe,' Ring replied.

'Anyway, how's Jam Tart? Have you spoken to him since all this?'

Jam! Ring couldn't believe he hadn't thought to call his friend. He hoped they still were friends. Surely an apology would sort it? Then again, he remembered some of the things he said, and the way he'd said them, and suddenly he felt like it wouldn't be as easy to repair that relationship as it had been with Sugar.

A job for tomorrow, he thought.

'Yeah, he's good. He's in journalism now. Came with me for my try-outs to document my story. I haven't spoken to him though. We sort of fell out after all this.'

'Oh, right. Well, let's hope he has another article planned then,' Ring's mum replied. 'And do you ever hear from Angel Slice? We always thought you two would end up together.' She giggled, a high-pitch *huhuhu* that she only ever did when talking about Angel.

'Nope, not heard from her since we broke up,' Ring said as coolly as he could muster.

'Oh, that is a shame. I tell you who I did see the other day out the front...'

Ring let the conversation wash over him, realising he was in for a very long rest of the day.

Day eight was meant to be the day he'd call Jam, but he kept getting distracted. Or finding distractions. The tin can sat on the side-table upstairs ominously, so he went downstairs to help out with the hotel.

He spent the morning helping Sugar with some filing, sorting out the mess under the front desk. They'd made a deal with Mum that they would work together to sort things out - but only if she made herself scarce for the day. They didn't need her micromanaging or undoing their progress.

After she'd left, Sugar, sporting a yellow custard wig today that rolled down her back, had given Ring a list of tasks to do, and he'd diligently set about completing them. Sure, Sugar had to re-do a couple, or had to show him how to do some of the newer jobs around the Doughchester, but he was good at lugging furniture about and putting up new paintings, and it was only after he'd done quite a lot of that that he realised his body was a bit sore but not unmanageable.

'That's not a fight injury, that's just because you've never worked hard before,' Sugar joked.

Ring woke up stiff and in pain on the ninth day after his scuffle, and the way he was moving was an 'eyesore', according to his mum, so he was relegated to staying up on the fifth floor.

He did go through a couple of his old boxes, making a pile of things to take back to his apartment - when was he going to go back there? - and a pile of things to throw away. Most things went into the throw away pile, old school books and clothes that he definitely wouldn't wear now.

In the keep pile: a Cassius Cake action figure, a series of other old notebooks about boxing, a family photo of the four of them outside the Doughchester Hotel, a completed FOOD FiGHT! sticker album, a couple of old t-shirts that he actually quite liked, a board game that he forgot he had, some other boxing video tapes, and a multi-coloured cube puzzle that he decided he would finally solve.

He got up and went to his desk to grab the red 'Strategies and tactics' notebook but realised it wasn't there. Opened the drawer and it wasn't there either.

'Where did I leave it, then?' He thought.

He looked for a bit but couldn't find it,

wondered if it had ever been there or if he'd simply conjured up the image of it in his battered and bruised state.

Besides, he had more boxes to go through. It wouldn't do to get too focused on one notebook.

In the end, he went through almost half of the boxes - which felt like enough of an achievement to drift off for a late afternoon nap. By the time he woke up, it was too late to do any of the other jobs he'd been putting off, so he sloped through to the lounge and watched old television shows with his mum.

She didn't say anything, but she smiled the whole time.

On day ten, he waited in the lounge for his mum and sister to wake up.

He was disappointed that it took them so long, actually. When he was younger, he was always the last to roll out of bed and he was mocked mercilessly because of it.

He was even more disappointed that, when they did get up, they didn't even notice what he'd done.

Should I just tell them? He thought, as Sugar began talking about what she was going to do with her morning off from work.

'Sorry, have neither of you noticed?' He

pointed.

Both shook their heads.

'Seriously? I shouldn't have bothered!' He smiled, but there was a tiny, tiny, tiny crumb of truth in that sentiment.

'It's too early for these games,' Sugar sighed.

'Well then it was definitely too early for me when I got up and fixed all the photos on the wonky wall earlier then, wasn't it?'

They both looked again, heads turning simultaneously towards the wall where all the photos were now lined up, perfectly straight. Or at least not noticeably wonky any more.

Sugar gasped.

A silence followed. A hand-over-mouth silence. A smiling eyes silence.

'Ring, that is amazing,' Sugar said, 'that's so kind of you.'

'Thank you, Ring,' Mum said, getting up to hug him, 'but I don't really see the difference.'

'You're kidding?' Sugar laughed.

'No, it's really kind and I'm sure you did do something but... Were they wonky before? They look the same as they did.'

'Were the photos on the wonky wall wonky? Where do you think the name came from, Mum?' Ring laughed, still squeezing her tight.

'You're a good son,' she said, and he could hear

the tears muffled against him.

'Oh, Mum, don't cry. He can put them back,' Sugar joked.

'No, I'm fine,' Mum said, sitting back down. 'It's just been so good to have you back, son. So good, so nice to have us all together again. I don't want it to end.'

Ring didn't know what to say. He hadn't really thought about going home lately, but he knew he'd need to at some point.

'Don't worry, Ring. I know you're overthinking what to say. I know you'll have to go back to your apartment. This was probably a leaving present, wasn't it?' She sniffed, a sad smile on her round face, behind her steamed lenses. 'You've been here a week and a half. But it's just been so lovely.'

'Well, yeah, I will have to go back to my place at some point but I wasn't planning to go today-' *When am I planning to go?*'-and, I was thinking, maybe I could come back and help out? Y'know, being as I don't have anything else going on at the moment. If that's ok?'

Another stream of fresh tears, a huge smile baked across her face. She leapt up to hug him again.

'He's not coming in at my level though, right, Mum? He would be junior to me? Right?' Sugar quizzed.

'Worry about that later,' she replied.

It was on the morning of the eleventh day that Ring decided to head back to his apartment.

He was due to start at the Doughchester Hotel tomorrow on 'light desk duties' according to his mum; or on 'general first day low-level grunt work' according to his sister, who insisted he call her 'Boss' in work hours.

Ring was taking a box of stuff from his 'keep pile' with him. He wanted to be clear that he wasn't coming to live back home, just to work there for a bit, and he felt this was the best way to symbolise that to his mum.

'Oh, you don't need to do that today, Ring. Why don't you just leave it and I'll send it over to you another time? Or you could stay here tonight, too? Shorten the commute.'

'I should check the place is still ok. The neighbours might be getting worried that nobody's been home in so long,' Ring laughed.

'I'll call you before your shift tomorrow, then. Make sure you feel well enough to start.'

'Mum, he's not a baby. *Sheesh*,' said Sugar.

'It's fine. It's probably a good idea. My sleep pattern isn't exactly normal at the moment.'

Ring left the fifth floor via the stairs. It was still

early, so no guests would see him slightly limping on his way out. Not that there were any to see him.

That'll all change when Sugar and I take the reins, he reminded himself. It was going to be a brave new vision, beginning tomorrow. Ring Doughnut was coming back and he was determined to make this hotel the success he always knew it could be.

The afternoon of the eleventh day was spent at his apartment.

A fine layer of dust covered absolutely everything, and his room was a lot tidier than he remembered it. He thought he'd left more stuff lying about, more ripped up posters and angst. In the end, it was just a bit unclean and dishevelled.

Ring looked over at the replica FOOD FiGHT! belt, sat proudly in the lounge. Even with the dust, it still shined with the outside light coming through the window, a glint on the corner of the gold faceplate.

I should give that to Mum to sell, he thought. It would probably have been worth more than his other boxing bits and pieces. Then again, they could display it in the lobby. Maybe make the Doughchester Hotel a sort of go-to lodgings for boxers and their entourage when in Alacrumba.

Ring ignored it for now, and instead set about

wiping down the surfaces and straightening out his furniture, and then began to unpack the box.

This was an ultimately fruitless task as the first thing he removed was the colourful cube puzzle, and he spent a good amount of time fiddling and faffing with it - though getting no closer to solving it.

Ring took a break from taking a break from unpacking, and decided to call Jam Tart. After a long time holding the line, the operator informed Ring that there was no answer.

'Would you like me to try again, Mr Doughnut? Over.'

'No, that's fine. Thank you,' Ring replied. 'Over and- Actually, are you the person I spoke to before? Over.'

'Sorry, I don't understand. Over.'

'A few days ago. I was… Shouting. Rude to you. At least, I think it was you. Am I right? Over.'

A pause. Then she answered, 'A couple of weeks ago. Yes. Over.'

Weeks? Of course. 'I wanted to say sorry. I had just had a… No, no excuses. I am sorry, Miss Operator. Over.' Ring found himself grinning, holding the can to his ear.

'I appreciate your apology, Mr Doughnut. Over.'

'Great. Over.'

'Is there anything else you need? Over.'

Now it was Ring's turn to pause.

'Erm, no. I suppose not. Thank you, and sorry again, and thank you. Over.'

'You're welcome. Over and out.'

What was that? He asked himself, slumping onto the sofa. He felt the heat rising in his cheeks, pushing his mouth into a goofy smile that wouldn't shift. Lightness across his body, giddiness in his head. He thought about who else he could call today. Briefly thought about Angel, weirdly.

That prompted him to go back to the boxes before he could sit and be silly for too much longer.

Naturally, he got distracted again.

After taking out the Cassius Cake action figure and putting it next to the replica belt - 'For now, until I find somewhere better for it' - and folding a couple of t-shirts up and putting them in a drawer, he was then looking for a smart place to put his notebooks.

He didn't really have any bookcases, and his options for storage were quite low. They could go on a shelf but they were a bit untidy. Well-worn and thumbed through. That wasn't the sort of vibe he was going for in his new life.

So, after circling the rooms in his apartment, he decided that, maybe, it was time to let them go. The information would be out of date by now and, besides, he wouldn't need to know any of it when he was helping to run the Doughchester.

Something gnawed at him in that moment. A peaceful emptiness, a stillness. Acceptance, perhaps.

'One last time, for all the good times,' he said, eyes welling up. *They're just notes, Ring! Pull it together.*

Still, he opened the first one - blue cover, slightly torn, titled 'Ring's Match Reports' - and he read his thoughts and feelings about "King" Cassius Cake versus a whole host of other boxers. He wrote three, four, five pages per match, detailing the strikes, the combinations, the knock-out punch. He even drew a little diagram of Cake's finishing manoeuvre, the "Birthday Bumps", and added notes on how he could achieve it. Notes that he actually had followed.

He was over half-way through the notebook before he got to a match that didn't directly involve Cassius Cake - though it was a match to determine the champion's next opponent, so his shadow still loomed large.

Ring put the notebook to one side, along with 'Ring's Match Reports II' and 'Ring's Match Reports III', and pulled out another.

He remembered this one clearly. Black front, no discernible markings. Held shut by a faded red rubber band.

This was his super-secret training regimen.

Opening it up, the first page was titled 'Road to Undisputed Training Plan', and it demanded that he do 100 sit-ups, 100 push-ups, 100 squats, and a 10 metre run every single day. How often had he completed that? He remembered sharing it with Granddough, who had told him he needed to focus a bit more of technique; had drawn up another training plan on the next page. That was their starting point.

A different feeling now: a murmur, a rumbling in the peaceful emptiness. A kernel of doubt. All those days he'd trained, he'd pursued the dream. Even though he was only going back to the Doughchester Hotel for a bit, something inside him wanted to know how long 'a bit' actually was - because whenever he thought about the future, he didn't see himself going on runs, or working the punchbag, or putting on a pair of gloves, or stepping between the ropes again. He had never gone two weeks without training before. What did that mean? Was that normal after a fight?

Ring put the notebook down in the pile with the others, and he closed the box.

'You've got to focus on the next day for now,' he said. 'You'll get back into it when you've recovered.' He hadn't convinced himself.

He thought of how happy his mum looked; how much easier it would make life for his sister. It would be good for him, too. All these notes, all of whatever this was: it was an obsession. An unhealthy obsession. A break would do them good; do him good, too.

Then he thought of his grandfather and the joy, the pride he had when they sparred. The way they'd stay up late to watch fights together and cheer on the "King". Could he leave it behind?

It's just for a bit. Just while you sort yourself out, he thought.

He nodded, resolving to tidy up his apartment for the rest of the afternoon and then relax for an evening ahead of his new start tomorrow.

A surprisingly good night's sleep on his broken bed heralded the beginning of day twelve after the clash with the cinnamon bun.

Day one of his new role as... Well, he didn't know his title officially. Co-manager? Assistant hotel manager? Whatever it was, he hoped it annoyed Sugar.

Ring Doughnut was up early and dressed in a smart white shirt and black trousers, with polished black shoes as well. He still had some marking on his face and he did the best to hide the other signs of the beating that were still there on his chest and body.

'It adds character,' he reassured himself.

Sure as anything, his mum called. The white string jumped and the can jangled gently.

'Good morning, Mr Doughnut. A call from the Doughchester Hotel. Do you accept? Over.' It was her again. Miss Operator. Ring smiled.

Forgot to answer.

'Mr Doughnut? Over.'

'Oh, yes. Good morning to you, too. How are you today? Over.'

'Ha, I'm fine Mr Doughnut. I'll put you through to the hotel now. Over and out.'

'Thank you!' He shouted, hoping he got that to her just in time.

The next voice he heard was his mum's.

'Hello, son. Are you ready for your first day? Over.' He could hear her happiness radiating down the line, almost singing the words as she spoke them.

'Yes, I'm just about to head down now. Thought I'd try to impress my new boss by turning up early. Over.'

They both chuckled.

'I'm sure they'll be very impressed with you. Did you have a nice evening? How was your apartment when you got back there? If you like, you could come home for tonight? Over.'

'Maybe, let's see if I survive the first shift,' Ring deflected. 'But yeah, it was nice to be back. Had some tidying up to do, went through some of my old things.' He paused. Ring knew he had something he wanted to say, but he didn't know how he'd say it.

In the end, the words fell out of his mouth.

'Mum, I wanted to say thank you for supporting me with boxing. I know you've always been clear you didn't like it and you wanted me to stop, but then I was reading all my notebooks and looking at all my stuff and it's just, like, well... It's all boxing. It's all I've ever focused on. And, I guess, it must have been hard for you, and even though you made your feelings perfectly clear, you still bought me the gloves and the shorts and the posters and the video tapes, and, yeah. Thank you. It didn't work out for me this time, but that's on me - not on you. Over.'

There was a silence between them.

'That's ok. That's what mothers do for their children.' Her voice was a whisper. 'Over.'

She's probably trying not to cry. Ring knew his mum wore her emotions close to the surface.

'I just want you to know that I know it must have been difficult. Anyway, I'll get a move on now. See you soon, Mum. Over and ou-'

'-Ring, wait. Wait. Are you still there? Over.'

'Yeah. Everything ok? Over.' *She sounds upset.*

For a long time, the line was quiet. Ring felt tense, his shoulders hunched, leaning into the tin can. He was breathing fast and shallow for some reason. His mind raced - was someone hurt? Did she not actually want him to work there? Had something happened? Had they gone out of business?

Finally, she spoke, and her voice was steady and cool, the emotion held back.

'If you had one more chance to box, to be a professional boxer, would you take it? Over.'

Yes. 'What like, FOOD FiGHT! level or just a local fighter around here? Over.'

'I don't know. But say you had the chance to have at least one professional bout. What would you do? Over.'

Take it. 'It's a tough question. I mean, it doesn't matter now anyway. I failed my try-out and I don't have any more lined up. Plus, my new job starts today. Why do you ask? Over.'

'But if you did. If you did have something lined up. A school or gym, or whatever, I mean. If you did, would you want to box again? Over.'

Even if it was just one fight and I lost it in the first round. 'What's going on, Mum? What aren't you telling me? Over.'

'We spoke, the day after you had that brawl

outside the hotel. I was so worried and so upset, you weren't even awake most of the time. But the moments when you were, you told me all about why you box. How it is your destiny, your dream. You spoke with such passion. Love, even.'

She paused, but Ring knew she wasn't done. He hadn't ever spoken to her properly about boxing because it always ended in an argument. He couldn't help but wonder how she'd reacted.

Finally, she spoke again: 'You know, your grandfather never wanted me to buy this hotel. He told me it would always be a struggle, a huge burden that I'd have to carry. A constant source of worry. He was right - oh, he was so right! - but he still helped me put down a deposit. Still helped to put together furniture and paint the rooms. Went all across the Doughjo picking up odd pieces I wanted to have here. He advised - but he never dictated, never decided. That was always up to me.' Another pause, a small sob that she stifled. Ring hoped Sugar was with her; imagined his sister holding her hand.

She continued, 'I miss him. So much. I wish he was still here.'

'Mum...' Ring whispered. He didn't know what to say. They didn't often mention Granddough to each other. Not anymore.

'He's here, though. If I let him. He's here in

who you have become. In who Sugar has become. He's here every time I use his wisdom - whether that be because I never buy a hotel again, or because I take a few parenting lessons from him. So come down to the hotel. We need to talk. I love you, son, and I'm proud of you too. Over and out.'

Ring Doughnut sat in the office behind the reception desk at the Doughchester Hotel. The sun had barely risen, and the orange glow it cast across the shop floor was only just creeping down over the glossy white exterior of the hotel.

The room was cool and crisp and dark. The desk which was normally covered in manila folders and stacks of papers had remained tidy from when he and Sugar had blitzed it the other day; the filing system still mostly in place, with just a couple of invoices on the floor.

Opposite: Ring's mum, sat in her big, comfy chair, a sad smile on her face. Her eyes were red and puffy behind her spectacles, but she looked strong in a powerful maroon jacket and her signature pearls. She nodded, reassured him.

Between them, on the almost-purple wooden desk, were two items.

A red notebook, entitled 'Strategies and Tactics by Ring Doughnut'.

A small, black, rectangular card with three

words scribbled in white pen.

'You're sure you're ok with this?' Ring asked again. The conversation had been short but heavy.

She nodded enthusiastically, flashed her teeth in a smile, dabbed at her eyes with a thick finger.

'I'm ok with it if it is what *you* want. Don't worry about me or your sister, or what your grandfather would have said. Do what *you* want.'

His pulse beat faster and his body was hot beneath the cool white shirt. What did Ring Doughnut want?

Ring picked up the tin can - it was painted a gold colour but had chipped, showing some of the burnished tin beneath. He spoke clearly down the line, to an operator who's voice he didn't recognise.

'Hi, could you connect me to-' Ring squinted, making out the characters, '-*Jacked Potato's Gym*, please? Over.'

'Of course, sir. Should I say it's a call from the Doughchester Hotel, or someone specific? Over.' The operator sounded far too awake and alert for this early in the morning. Maybe he had received some big news as well.

'Ring Doughnut,' he replied, then added, 'the one who he stopped from getting beaten up. Over.'

The operator snorted. It *was* a weird way to refer to yourself, Ring supposed.

After the longest 'one moment' Ring had ever experienced, which included several anxious, awkward glances with his mum and a series of strange facial expressions that probably didn't convey how either of them was really feeling, a voice came on the other end of the phone.

'Ah, kid! I was wondering when you'd call. Playing hard to get. So, you want to give it a go then, do ya?' His voice was deep, direct, somehow comforting. He spoke quickly, a ferocious pace that seemed at odds with his voice. 'Kid? You there?'

'Yes, sorry. Yes, I'm interested. But first, would it be ok if I asked you a question? I just wanted to know: why me? Why not the one who actually won the fight? Over.' Ring stammered, felt his tongue was too thick for his mouth.

'Who said he won? From what I saw, you outboxed him. Had that won on points easily. Only problem for you was the big oaf just tackled you. Well, that and the fact that you tried to win on points in a street brawl. Lesson one: remember the context of the fight.' The voice on the other end laughed heartily.

I suppose he did cheat, Ring agreed.

'Now, I've got a question for you, kid. You've got huge potential and, with the right trainer, you can go a long way. What we need to find out is if I'm the right trainer for you - and to do that, I'm going to ask you one question. No pressure, and don't try and be smart and tell me the right answer either. I'll know. Got it?'

'Yes. Over.'

'Good - but that wasn't the question, either. So, I suppose I've got a second question, actually,' he laughed again, and Ring felt a smile spread across his face that caused his mum to issue an unconvincing thumbs up that he waved off. 'The question is: why do you want to be a boxer?'

Ring didn't hesitate, didn't even wait for the 'over' that he now understood was never going to come down the line: 'I want to become FOOD FiGHT! Champion. Over.'

'Ha! You and everyone else. So, FOOD FiGHT! gets a new champion. Why does that matter to you?'

Had Ring answered incorrectly? He took his time on the follow-up; realised he was taking too long when Mum grimaced at the silence.

'It would show I'm the best boxer. I want the legacy that Cassius Cake has, so I guess I want people to remember me. Over.'

'Don't guess, kid. When you get hit in the face, you're going to need to *know* exactly why you're being punched if you wanna get back up. Why do you want to be remembered?'

Ring looked at his mum, who nodded.

Mouthed 'go on' to him. Ring shrugged. She nodded again, her face straining with desperation to provide him with an answer she didn't have.

'I'm going to be a boxer because it will always connect me to my grandfather. He trained me right up until he... Well, until he couldn't any more. He's always with me, but never more so than when I'm boxing. I won't give up because he won't let me. I want the championship for myself - but I want to box for him.' He felt his face flush, his body go hot, his eyes dampened - but he was glad to have said it out loud. Mum was gripping his hand tightly, smiling as wide as she possibly could under steamed up spectacles. 'Over.'

'Kid, I love it. Make no mistake: you're gonna be an underdog, and it sure ain't gonna be easy. We'll have to work hard and you'll need to commit everything to this, got it? But I'm willing to grind our way to the top if you are. So, I'm in. What d'ya say? Are you in?'

Ring was somewhere else. He was in that front room. The green chairs and sofas, the red wine carpet. The sound of the television. Granddough in his chair. A smile on his face. A boxing match on the big screen rendered in colour, but it wasn't one Ring recognised. Not yet, anyway.

'Kid?'

'Hi, yeah, sorry. I'm in. I'm all in! Over.' Ring

smiled and his mum squeezed his hand and shook his arm with both hands.

'Phew! You kept me waiting there, worried you might've had a change of heart,' he laughed, a raucous sound that seemed to come from some chaotic depth. 'You start in two days from now. Find us at Jacked Potato's Gym in Mississipie. You'll spot us easily enough.'

Ring had never heard of it, but he didn't care. Being in a gym and having a coach was his route into boxing, into FOOD FiGHT! events, into securing a legacy for himself - and for his grandfather.

The first step towards "King" Cassius Cake and the FOOD FiGHT! Championship.

'Who should I ask for? Over.'

'Name's Coach Potato - and we're gonna go to the very top, kid.'

Ring Doughnut's journey continues in
FOOD FiGHT! Volume 2.

Available March 2025.

Roll with the Punches

Bonus Chapter

Roly Poly stood outside his front door for a good while; would probably have stayed out there the entire afternoon and evening if his wife, Jolie, hadn't noticed and ushered him in.

The banner that was draped from the windows had "You can do it! Good luck!" written in red crayon, a jumble sale of capital and lowercase letters.

'How did it go?' Jolie whispered, although her eyes told him that she already knew.

'I didn't make it,' Roly said. 'But I'm fine with it, honestly.'

'Oh, honey,' Jolie said, kissing him on the side

of his face, squeezing his log-shaped body so the cream and jam filling squirted out of his nose a little. 'You can always apply again, right?' She smiled.

He loved that smile.

That smile had won him over when he was just a young sponge roll in the Doughjo, barely knowing what life would look like outside of Calorifornia.

That smile had forced him to overcome his embarrassment and ask her on a date that went so well that they had another and another, and eventually set a day for a wedding, and had a beautiful son, Junior.

That smile had always been there when he spoke of his dreams of doing something that wasn't washing windows, when he spoke about how he wouldn't mind trying his hand at FOOD FiGHT!. When his applications to top gyms and bottom gyms and all the gyms in the middle failed year after year, the smile never gave up, never lost hope.

That smile was how he knew he was happy he tried, and content with the outcome.

'No, I think that's enough of that,' Roly said, a final tight squeeze back to his wife. 'Honestly, Jolie, some of those boxers aren't even half my age and they're so fast and so competent - I couldn't have kept up.'

'Oh, stop it. Of course you could.'

'No, honestly, I'm not being modest. The youngsters want it more. My trial had me and another older guy, and these two who can't have been baked all that long ago. Well, this lad, a doughnut, he was so zoned in. I found myself half-watching him, to be honest. He wanted it so badly, you know? Needed it. It was amazing. It also made me realise that I… Well, I just didn't want it. I don't need it.' *I don't need it*, he said again to himself. He scoffed at the revelation.

'If you're sure and you're really happy, then I won't be upset to have you around a bit more again, now you'll be doing less training.'

'I didn't say I'd train less. You don't want me to lose these, do you?' He flexed his arms, admiring the thickness and definition of them.

Jolie squeezed them, shook her head. 'Maybe I can make some sacrifices, then.'

They walked through towards the back of the house and Roly put his gym gear away. He appreciated how tidy the house was, understood the effort it took for both of them - especially when he remembered how messy they both were in their youth. That first apartment, over in Mississipie, had been an atrocity. Clothes everywhere, no storage, no two shoes left in the same place. They'd come a long way together. Still had a long way to go.

'How do you think Junior's going to react?' That was the bit Roly was dreading.

He didn't want to disappoint his son, which is why he never had. He'd worked hard building out his own business washing windows for the rich and glamorous of Calorifornia, then managed to schmooze his way into cleaning the big window at the front of the shop for a ridiculous number of tokens that helped them buy a great house in the suburbs and have all the latest toys and gadgets. He had managed to employ his brother and his sister to help him, and even had Jolie part-time running the books. Junior never wanted for anything, although he knew the value of what he had, that much Roly was insistent on.

'Oh, he'll be ok. He's proud of his dad for even being selected to go,' Jolie said in a hushed voice.

Roly could hear Junior playing in the lounge. It sounded like he was acting out a boxing match, mimicking the roar of the crowd and the ebb and flow of a fight. He could imagine his son, his spitting image really, a golden sponge rolled tightly, swirled with white cream and jam, flinging himself onto the sofa then leaping back to his feet, tearing over to the other side of the room.

'You sure? He gave me a grilling last night about it. I was worried he already had his heart set on me getting in.'

'He's a kid, Roly. This week he dreams of you being a big-name boxer; next week it'll be an athlete or one of those suits in Bisconsin.' They both laughed at the thought of Roly in a suit, strutting around with all the biscuits.

'I know, I know. Here's hoping he wants his dad to be a window washer one day, eh?'

'Or he might want to be an accountant like his mother?' Jolie grinned.

'Is anyone else here? I thought my mum and dad might pop by?' Roly asked.

'No, no, just us. I told them to stop by later. I can call them and tell them to cancel, if you're not in the mood?'

'Jolie, I'm fine. Call them up. Tell them we're celebrating tonight. I achieved my dream.'

'Of trying out?' She was still smiling, still supportive. He loved that about her, wanted to hold her tight and tell her a thousand times how much he loved her.

'Of having a family.'

Jolie pulled a face, pretended to be disgusted, grinning the whole time. They kissed, a long, lingering kiss, before she broke off the embrace and told him to stop being so cringe-worthy and stop putting off telling Junior.

'I'll call your mum and dad and tell them to

come over whenever, then I might just pop out to the shops quickly,' she said.

'Sounds good. I'll catch you a bit later then,' Roly said.

'Great. Love you, honey.'

'I love you, too.'

Roly Poly stood outside the door to the lounge, listening to his son.

The fight had obviously concluded, though Roly couldn't tell who the winner was or in what fashion it had ended. Junior had moved on to another game, but it was one he was playing out quietly, his imagination not requiring quite the same stage as it had before.

He was about to go in when he heard a conversation Junior was having with himself in voices that were meant to be different people but sounded remarkably similar.

'That'll be five tokens please.'

'My windows have never been so clean. Have ten tokens for doing such a good job.'

Jolie was right, Roly thought, realising how obvious that statement was the moment it entered his head.

He pushed open the door.

'Dad!' Junior jumped up and ran over to Roly, hugging his dad around the waist. 'Did you win?'

Roly Poly hugged his son, then crouched down to his level. Junior had his mother's face, her optimism.

'Well, before all that, have you had a good day so far?' He said.

'Yeah, I was just playing and watched some TV with Mum. She said granny and gramps are coming over later, too, so I had to tidy my room.'

'Wow, that sounds like an action-packed day, kiddo.'

'So, did you win? Are you going to be in FOOD FiGHT!?'

Roly Poly fell back into a sitting position, legs out in front of him. He was eye-to-eye with Junior now and he could see the excitement, the sparkle. Heard it in his voice.

Roly remembered what Jolie had said to him.

'Son, I tried really hard but I didn't make it,' he said, nodding his head for some reason.

'Oh...'

'I hope you're not disappointed. I really did try my best but everyone there was so good.'

Junior jumped at Roly, hugged him. Sniffed a little.

'It's ok, Dad. Don't be sad,' Junior said, his voice muffled.

'Hey, I'm not sad. I gave it a good shot but it wasn't to be - and that's ok.'

'It's just Mum said that this was your dream from when you were my age.'

'Ha! It was, it was. But dreams can change. Sometimes the things you wanted yesterday aren't the things that you will want tomorrow.' Roly played the sentence back to himself in his head and couldn't decide whether that was very wise or nonsense. He liked it, anyway; made a note to say it to Jolie later and gauge her reaction.

'I don't know what my dream is yet,' Junior said. 'How would I know what it is?'

'Hmm, good question.' *How did I know?* 'Ok, let's try something. You shut your eyes really tight. Tighter than that, so you can't see anything.'

'Ok.'

'Ok, now, think of something that makes you really happy.'

'Yeah.'

'What is it that you saw?'

'All my toys,' Junior replied earnestly.

'Ok,' Roly stifled a laugh. 'So now maybe try and think about something that you don't have. Something that would make you happy.'

'Like new toys?'

'I guess so, or it could be something that you can't really touch.'

'What do you see, Dad?'

Roly didn't need to shut his eyes, but he did so

anyway. Immediately, it flashed up: his family, in front of their house. Over his shoulder was a ladder and one of his little yellow buckets by his feet. He was proud. And sure, somewhere, there was still the tiniest thought of him in a boxing ring, but it wasn't him now. It was a younger Roly Poly, a dream from someone else.

'I see you and your mum, and Granny and Gramps, and I see us all smiling and playing games in the garden.'

'That's not a proper dream. That's just a normal day.' Junior said, opening his eyes. He was disappointed.

Roly laughed. He stood up and hoiked Junior into the air, onto his shoulders. He briefly panicked, realising that his son's head nearly thumped into the roof. Junior was giggling though.

'Then here's a dream for you: my son, Roly Poly Junior, winning the FOOD FiGHT! Championship - and I'm his coach! The greatest ever father and son team. How's that for a good dream?'

'Yeah! We'll win it together!' Junior raised his arms, this time hitting the ceiling. They both laughed. 'And I'll beat whoever it was that beat you today as well.'

'That doughnut won't stand a chance,' Roly

said, bumping fists with Junior before lowering him down. He thought about telling him he'd lost in the preliminary tests, that he hadn't actually got in a ring, that he hadn't thrown a punch at anyone - but Junior was already acting out the championship round, bouncing off of the sofa and throwing what could only be described as some unorthodox punches.

There was a knock at the door.

'Granny and Gramps!' Junior shouted, running out of the room.

'They got here quickly,' Roly said to himself.

'Hey, we're in the lounge,' he heard Junior say to them, 'I'm practicing my boxing. I'm going to be FOOD FiGHT! Champion. Dad's going to train me.'

He's got my ambition alright, Roly thought, tidying away a couple of toys by bundling them towards the wooden chest in the corner. He did enjoy it when his parents remarked on how tidy the place was. It gave him a chance to pass the credit on to Jolie - which she did deserve the bulk of anyway.

'Is he now? Did he get in then?' Granny replied.

'No, he lost to a doughnut. But I won't lose to anyone. I'm going to be the best ever.'

Roly smiled.

I wonder how that doughnut kid did in the end?

Author's Note

I hope you had as much fun reading about Ring Doughnut's first foray in boxing as I have writing it (and Frank has editing it). The aim of FOOD FiGHT! has always been to find a balance between silly and substantial. As the story goes on, I plan to pack in a sizeable portion of puns alongside a hefty helping of the heavy stuff.

As for how long the story goes on, well, who knows? My intention is to write these in a serialisation, not dissimilar from manga and comics. I've got the first arc lined up and that's four volumes of story, as a fairly reliable estimate, and then there are two further arcs plotted out, each around a similar length. I'm sure at some point my website will include some more detail there. So, basically, stick with me and enjoy the ride - you never know who might turn up next.

Some characters here are inspired by the food I saw and subsequently ate over the course of writing this book (sorry, Jam Tart). Others came to life as a way to pay tribute to my loved ones.

The most obvious example is Granddough,

who is a not-so-subtle tribute to my own Grandad, who passed away ten years ago. The relationship between Ring and Granddough is not exactly the same as David and Grandad, but it does share a desire from the grandson to make their grandfather proud - whether that's through throwing punches or delivering punchlines.

While I will never know if I've achieved my goal in relation to my Grandad, I know that Granddough would be very pleased with Ring's early progress, setbacks and all, and he'd be chuffed to bits with what's to come for our dough-eyed dreamer in Volume 2.

I look forward to seeing you there!

David Butteridge, August 2024.

@davidbutteridge
r/TheDoughjo

PS: If you've enjoyed FOOD FiGHT! Volume 1, please consider leaving a review to help others find their way to the Doughjo!

About the Author

David Butteridge was born in Lincolnshire. He graduated with a First Class Bachelor's degree in Journalism with Creative Writing from the University of Chester. David now writes from the south-coast in England, where he is ably assisted by his dachshund, Frank. In an ideal world, David would only ever need to eat sandwiches and pizza. FOOD FiGHT! Volume 1 is his first novel.